PRA
JACK DA
MAGLL

Arf arf arf arf ARF arf arf ARF!
(Scabby earlobes, this book is AMAZING. Don't be a
scaredy sock and read it NOW.)
Opi, aged 10

'Original, brilliant and as funny as a pig on stilts!
Jack Dash is my kind of hero.'
Matt Brown, author of *Compton Valance*

'There's mayhem, there's madness, there's even a pet
sea lion! The world of Jack Dash is great fun!'
Ruth Fitzgerald, author of *Emily Sparkes*

'Thoroughly entertaining, exciting, funny and
imaginative – and I love the use of language
and place names. Brilliant!!'
Giles Andreae, author of *Billy Bonkers*

'It is funny with a capital 'F'!
Jack Dash and the Magic Feather is a crazy, clever
carnival ride of a story. Bonkers, brilliant and
feather-tastic! You had me at 'Oi! Dozy Knickers!'.
Mo O'Hara, author of *My Big Fat Zombie Goldfish*

JACK DASH
AND THE
SUMMER BLIZZARD

By
SOPHIE PLOWDEN

Illustrated by
Judy Brown

FOR MY MOTHER,
WITH LOVE

CATNIP BOOKS
Published by Catnip Publishing Ltd
320 City Road
London
EC1V 2NZ

This edition first published 2017
10 9 8 7 6 5 4 3 2 1

A CIP catalogue record for this book is available from
the British Library.

ISBN 978-1-91061-106-7

www.catnippublishing.co.uk

'*I am not always good and noble. I am the hero of this story, but I have my off moments.*'

– P.G. Wodehouse, *Love Among the Chickens*

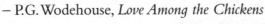

oNE

A rattle . . . a clink . . . the scrape of a key . . .

Jack Dash huddled in the darkness, pulling his knees as tight as they'd go. *Dubba-dub, dubba-dub,* his heart was thumping and the back of his neck prickled with sweat. *Stay calm,* he told himself. *Just keep quiet and they'll go away.*

Clatter – clink – clank.

What was that? Jack held his breath and screwed his eyes shut. *Please, please, please – make them go away. I'll eat my Brussels sprouts and I'll wash my neck and I'll never stuff my dirty socks down the back of the fridge again.*

'Jack?'

'Don't touch me,' he gasped.

'Jack, it's me.'

Five icy fingers seized him by the arm. Jack tried to wrench it free but the fingers tightened. And then came a laugh – it tore through his skull like a high-speed train, rising to a screech that sent his hair electric.

'Let me go, you brute! You fiend! You . . . you terrapin!' With a twist of his elbow Jack yanked his arm away. 'Aaarrggh!' he yelled, falling backwards into the black – waving and tipping and kicking and sliding and –

Thump!

'Dumpling, it's me.'

'Huh?'

'It's me. Mum.'

'*Mum?*' Jack sat up and rubbed his eyes. Sure enough, Mrs Dash was looming over him, hands on her hips and top lip twitching. 'I – I don't understand,' he said. 'Where am I? What's going on?'

'You fell out of bed, you silly sausage! Up you get — it's eight o'clock. Time to get dressed.'

Jack blinked his bedroom back into focus — his jeans in a heap beside him . . . his gladiator shield and harpoon set . . . his ground-to-air rapid-fire doughnut blaster and his collection of toy cars — all scattered across the floor.

'I . . . I must've been dreaming.' He rubbed his head. 'It was terrible, Mum — someone was coming after me. They had me by the bicep. They were trying to . . .'

'Oh dear, oh dear, oh dear.' Mrs Dash was looking around the room. 'What a mess it is in here! And Jackie, your *hair.*

Don't forget to brush it – you look like a wild animal! You've got to be smart on your first day of school.'

'But I – I can't go!' Grasping the edge of his bed, Jack dragged himself to his feet. 'See? I can't even stand up properly! I've had the great-great-grandmother of all nightmares and my knee caps are still shaking from shock.'

'Hurry up,' said Mrs Dash, heading for the door.

'Mum – wait!'

'Breakfast's ready,' she called from the stairs. 'Mustn't be late.'

My very first day in a brand-new school . . .
Jack stared out of his bedroom window, his dream still thundering around his head. *And that laugh! It was worse than Mum when she's on the phone.* He shuddered. He could practically smell the danger. *It must have been some kind of warning,* he thought. *I might get locked in the lost-property cupboard . . . chopped up into tiny pieces . . . fed to a starving cockroach.* He raised his face to the sky. *I gotta get out of here – and fast.*

Up, up, up, high in the blue, a bird soared over Curtly Ambrose – above the rooftops and the treetops and the distant hills, tilting into the horizon. *If only I could fly away too,* thought Jack.

And then he remembered his magic feather.

Jack sat down at his rickety desk and opened the lid with a creak. He smiled to himself as it all came back to him — the moment he'd found the feather on the day they'd moved to Curtly Ambrose. Six days, nineteen hours and twenty-two minutes ago exactly. He remembered the first time he'd stepped inside his bedroom — the sunlight on the dusty floorboards . . . the smell of stale biscuits . . . the old wooden desk in the corner, tucked beneath the window . . . the strange glow shining through the gap under its lid. He remembered how he'd held his breath as he slid his hand inside.

Jack snapped himself back into the present. Slowly, carefully, he lifted out a book – it was old and heavy and bound in dark green leather. And just like the first time, he laid it on the desk and opened its ancient cover. There his feather, shimmering on the page. It was long. It was gold. It was curling. Its tip was stained with ink. It sparkled and fizzed as he twirled it in his hand.

Anything, he thought. *I can draw anything I want and — zap — it will come to life!* Jack rested his chin in his hand. *I could draw a plane with a private cinema. Reclining seats . . . surround-sound speakers . . . and a never-ending supply of sugar-coated pretzels.* He shook his head. *A plane's no good cos I don't have a pilot's licence.* He chewed his lip. *Perhaps I'll draw a kite*, he thought. *A kite so big it'll carry me away . . . except I might get hit by a thermal and blown over the tundra.*

'Ha!' he cried. 'A jetpack! I'll draw a one-person jetpack with twin turbine rockets and I'll strap it to my back and zoom-zoom-zoom over the town — higher than a spaceship and faster than the speed of light.' He ran to his cupboard to find his winter clothes. 'Better dress up warm. It's gonna be cold up there in the stratosphere.'

Dubba-dub, dubba-dub, Jack's heart was pounding. He sat down at his desk again, winding a scarf around his neck and tugging a hat over his ears. He picked up his feather and pressed it to the paper: in a thin black line, he drew a tube with a pointed top. Beside it he drew another. *Those are the booster tanks . . . now for the thrust.* And – *scratch-scratch, squiggle-scratch* – he added exhaust fumes underneath.

'Perfect. I'll be over the Atlantic and in Miami by teatime.' Jack scrunched his eyes shut. *Come on, feather – do your magic!*

Clink-clank!

Jack opened his eyes – there on his desk

stood a pair of rockets – smooth and shiny and gleaming white. 'Huh?' He scratched his eyebrow. He shook his head. 'They're . . . they're tiny!' He poked one with his finger. 'That's definitely not a one-person jetpack – it's a pair of salt and pepper pots.'

Clink-clink-clink – the pots began to wobble. **Clink-clank-clink** – they rattled and shook.

Jack jumped up. He backed away. Smoke was seeping from their bases. He coughed. He spluttered. He flapped his hand. The smoke was billowing towards him now in thick white clouds, stinging his eyes and burning his throat like hot jalapeño sauce. He ran to the window and pushed it open.

ZIP - CRACKLE - ZAP!

'Sweet jumping jelly beans – what was that?' Jack spun round and reeled backwards, shielding his eyes with his hand – two balls of fire, the size of his fists, were hovering over the desk. A shower of sparks sprayed on to the floor as they shot towards the ceiling.

WHOOOOSH! WHOOOOSH! BANG! BANG!

Jack rubbed his ears. He wiped his eyes. He studied the scorch mark on his desk . . . the smudges up the wall . . . the salt and pepper pots stuck in the plaster above his head, their bases still trickling smoke.

He looked at his feather on the floor. 'Well, smother me in butter and call me toast – it's never done that before!'

'Dumpling!' Jack's mother was shouting up the stairs.

No, no, no!

'What's going on up there?' she called. 'What's all that noise?'

Jack staggered on to the landing. 'I'll be down in a minute,' he yelled. 'Just dusting the furniture!' He ran back inside and snatched up his feather.

But first I'm going to hide this where no one will ever find it.

tWo

'Come along,' said Dad. 'Eat up!'

'I'm not hungry,' said Jack, dangling his spoon over his cornflakes.

'Dumpling, your *face*.' Mum put down her teacup and pulled out her hanky. 'What have you been doing? It's absolutely filthy.' She leaned across the table and dabbed at his cheek. 'And what's that stuff all over your shirt? You can't go to school looking like that.'

'What's the point of going at all? It's practically the summer holidays.' Jack tugged his scarf tight and shivered. 'I think it's safer if I stay at home and we can see how I feel in the autumn.'

'I've had enough of this,' said Mr Dash, folding up his newspaper. 'It wasn't easy to get you that place. You're going to school and that's that.'

Cock-a-doodle-doo! went the front doorbell.

'At last,' said Mum, scurrying into the hall. 'That'll be Coco.'

Jack swallowed. *Things are getting worse by the millisecond.* Coco McBean was the girl who lived next door, but Jack called her The Fruitcake. She knew all about Jack's feather and she wasn't afraid to use it.

Slam! and into the kitchen skidded The Fruitcake in a pair of tangerine trainers.

Her curly red hair was tied in pigtails, pointing at ten to four.

'Howdy-doody, Mr D,' she said, helping herself to a slice of Mr Dash's toast. 'What's up, Jack? You look terrible.' She wiped the crumbs off her chin with the back of her hand and peered into his face. 'You've gone all yellow like my granny's toenails.'

'He's always pale on Mondays,' said Mum, patting Jack on the head. 'But he's absolutely fine – aren't you, Dumpling?'

'No, I'm not. I'm not fine at all. In fact, I think I might expire in the next five minutes.' Jack could feel his mother's hand on the small of his back, steering him into the hall.

'Now, have you got everything?' Mrs Dash was reaching for the front door. 'Pencil case? Reading book?' She handed him his lunch box. 'I've made your favourite sandwich — pickled haddock with sliced banana.' She was turning the handle now. 'You won't be needing that hat, sweetie — it's going to be hot and sunny all week.'

'Mum, *please* . . .' Jack said, clinging to her sleeve. 'You — you can't do this. I'm your only child.'

'Everyone feels nervous when they start a new school.' She gave his cheek a cheerful tweak. 'I'm sure Coco will look after you. Won't you, Coco? . . . *Coco?* Oh dear — where's that girl got to now?'

'Right here, Mrs D!' *Thump — thump — thump* — Coco was coming down the stairs, three at a time, twizzling her pigtail and grinning.

It's a good job I've hidden my feather, thought Jack, *cos if The Fruitcake got her hands on it, she'd send us both into orbit.*

tHREE

'Don't worry,' said Coco, as they set off down Quarantine Street in the morning sunshine. 'I've got it.'

'Got what?' said Jack.

'Your feather, you dim-bat. It's in my backpack.'

'My magic feather?' Jack stopped walking. He turned to her and gawped. 'You're joking, right?'

'Nope. I found it in your bedroom.'

'You went into my *bedroom*?' Jack could feel his cheeks burning.

'Yep,' said Coco. 'I ran upstairs while

your mum was banging on and there it was – under your bed, hidden in a football sock and locked inside a box. First place I looked.' She shuffled off her backpack, dumped it on the pavement and rubbed her palms together. 'So what are we waiting for? I've got some paper in here somewhere . . .'

'Hang on!' said Jack, grabbing her hand.

Coco lifted her freckled face and stared at him. 'What d'you mean *hang on*?'

'I mean *stop*. I mean w*ait*. I mean *hold it right there.*' Jack checked over his shoulder and stepped in close. 'That feather is the most remarkable supernatural phenomenon known to humankind, and you want to use it? Right here? In the middle of Quarantine Street? No way, Coco. Not in a billion light years.'

'Who cares where we are? It's gonna be even more fun than cutting my dad's hair.'

'I'm being serious,' said Jack. 'Deadly serious. If we're not careful, we could end up in trouble right up to our armpits.'

Coco crinkled her forehead. 'What's got into you, flat-pants? That feather is the best thing ever and we haven't used it for two whole days.'

'I – er . . . I had a bit of an incident this morning, okay?'

'Really?' Coco grinned. 'Is that why your bedroom stank like a barbecue?'

Jack stuck out his hand. 'Just give it back, will you? We can't afford to take any risks – it's acting really strange at the moment.'

''S'funny,' said Coco. 'It was working fine just now.'

'Just now?' said Jack, scratching his head. 'What d'you mean *just now*?'

'Huk-huk!'

Jack stiffened. 'What was that?' he said, looking up and down the street.

'HAAARK!'

'Blinking Noreen – it's coming from in

there!' Jack pointed at Coco's backpack, which was lying at their feet. 'Something's inside it.' He took a step back. 'D–did you see that, Coco? It's *moving*!'

The bag rocked backwards and forwards then toppled over on to the pavement – something black and shiny was pushing up the flap.

'It's alive,' Jack squawked, 'and it's trying to get out!'

FOUR

'Okay, Coco – let's rewind. You went into my bedroom. You took my magic feather. And you drew a *penguin*?'

'Isn't he adorable?' Coco beamed at the creature squatting on the pavement – he was small and black like a bowling pin, with a round white tummy and a long orange beak. 'We'll call him Pablo – what d'you think?'

'Huk-huk!' Pablo looked at Jack and waggled his tail.

'Go on, then,' said Coco. 'Say hello.'

Jack crouched down to pat the penguin's head. 'Ow!' he yelped. 'He bit me!'

'Maybe he's a bit confused,' said Coco. 'He's only been here ten minutes.'

'*HAAARRK!*' screeched Pablo, shuffling in circles on his orange feet – faster and faster – arching his neck and flapping his wings.

'*A bit confused?*' said Jack, edging away. 'He's completely and utterly demented. He's probably got diseases – like chickenpox or goose bumps or pigeon toes. Uh-oh! What's he doing now?'

Peck-peck-peck – Pablo's head was inside the backpack and – 'Heeurrccch!' – he spat out a rubber on to the pavement.

'Right,' said Jack. 'We need a plan of action – we have a dangerous penguin running riot. What are we gonna do with it?'

'Take him to school, of course.'

'Are you out of your freckled mind? Did they actually swap your brain with a cucumber?' Jack buried his face in his hands. 'This is a fiasco and it's all your fault.'

'Chill out, chicken-knickers — it'll be a blast!'

'Chicken-knickers? Did you call me *chicken-knickers*?' Jack puffed out his chest and jabbed it with his thumb. 'This is Jumping Jack Dangerous you're talking to — I'm a professional wrestler, you know. I'm invincible. I'm untouchable. I eat wine gums for breakfast.'

'So what are we waiting for, Jumping J D? Is Pablo coming or what?'

Jack sighed. 'Okay,' he said. 'Let's do it.'

'*Yess!*' cried Coco, punching the air.

'But we've got to be extra-mega-careful. It's my first day, Coco. And I don't want any trouble — cos if the teachers found out . . .' Jack closed his eyes and swallowed.

'Pablo's our secret. Keep him in your backpack and don't show him to anyone. Anyone at all. Got it?'

'Careful. Teachers. Secret. Got it.'

'And don't use my feather again.'

Coco squeezed his arm and shivered. 'I can't wait. You, me and Pablo – we're going to have the best fun ever.'

FIVE

'This is it.' Coco stopped beside an iron gate set in a high brick wall. 'Curtly Ambrose School!'

Jack squished his face against the railings. He gazed up at the crumbling red bricks . . . the taped-up windows . . . the bush sprouting out of the gutter. 'Are you *sure*?'

'Course I'm sure, you numb-bum. I've been coming here since I was four years old.'

DONG!

The bricks shook, the windows rattled and a roof tile clattered to the ground.

'What was *that*?' said Jack, staggering back.

'The school bell.' Coco nodded at the clock tower with its arched window and pointed roof. 'Frostbite says if we ever go up there, she'll make sure we never come back.'

'*Frostbite?* Who's Frostbite?'

'The head teacher. Uh–oh, better shift it – she's right over there.' **Ker-chang!** Coco heaved the gate open. 'White face. Witchy fingers. Can't miss her.'

A woman was standing by the front door – long and lean, in an ice-blue suit and spiky silver shoes, with short sharp hair that shone like a helmet. A line of children was queuing up the steps – she grabbed the

first one by the ear, hauled him on to his
tiptoes and shone a torch into his mouth.

'W-what's she doing?' Jack whispered.

'Tooth Inspection,' said Coco. 'If she finds a wobbly one she'll pull it out with her pliers.'

'No way.' Jack swallowed. 'She – she can't do that!'

'It's true. Damien in Pluto Class told me – she did it to his sister.'

Miss Frostbite let the boy drop and waved him through the front door with a flick–flick–flick of her hand.

'And you should see her when she's angry,' said Coco. 'Her nostrils wobble and her lips go blue and I'll tell you something scarier – she can hypnotise you with her eyes. She stares and stares till she sucks you in and then she zaps you under.'

Jack gulped. He could feel his knees going weak. 'Coco,' he said, 'I think we should—'

'You're late!' Jack spun round. Miss Frostbite was towering above them, tapping her watch with a purple fingernail. 'Twenty-three seconds past nine, Miss McBean — that's a one pound fine, if I'm not mistaken.'

Uh-oh. She was staring at Coco's backpack now. *No, no, no* — it was bulging and squirming.

'Stop fidgeting, girl! Stand up straight or I'll scrub off your freckles with a scourer.' Miss Frostbite turned to look at Jack — her eyes narrowed to two blue slits. 'Who are you?'

Look away, thought Jack, *before she zaps me.*

'Speak up, boy – I can't hear you!'

'Huk!' went Coco's backpack.

Miss Frostbite's nostrils quivered. She glared at Coco. 'Did I ask you? No, Miss McBean, I did not. Go to your classroom and get out of my sight!' She flick-flicked her hand and Coco was gone. 'Answer the question, boy – what is your name?'

'J-Jack,' he said, gazing at her pointed toes. 'Jack Alphonse Exeter Dash.'

'Never heard of you,' she said. 'Go home.'

'But . . .'

'This is my school. I make the rules. You can't just turn up with your scruffy hair and your half-chewed nails, expecting an education.' She pointed at the gate. 'You heard me. Leave!'

Don't worry, thought Jack. *I'm off.*

But as he turned to run, five bony fingers grabbed his collar. 'Not so fast . . .' Miss Frostbite hauled him back towards her. 'Did you say your name was *Dash*? Are you the son of Lionel Dash? The new mayor of Curtly Ambrose?'

Jack nodded.

'Well, well, well − perhaps we've been a bit hasty.' Miss Frostbite curled her lip and bared her teeth like a wolf. 'Tell me something,' she said, winding her witchy fingers together. 'Does your father have a gold chain?'

Jack nodded again.

'Oh, that's *wonderful*!' Miss Frostbite purred, breathing coffee in his face. 'We must have a party to welcome him.' She was smiling at Jack now. 'Yes! A summer fair – with games and prizes and goodies and cakes and won't that be utterly delightful? I'll phone your father straight away.' She patted her hair and brushed down her skirt. 'Now, hurry along – you're in Neptune Class with that . . . that *girl*.' She twirled her nail at the front door. 'It's down there somewhere. You'll find it.'

Jack walked down the long dark corridor — it smelt of sweaty cabbage and boiled socks. The paint on the walls was peeling and the strip lights flickered and buzzed.

Saturn Class . . . Jupiter Class . . . Uh-oh. The sign on the next door said *Neptune Class.* Jack felt his tummy twist. He reached for the handle. His hand was shaking. He could hear noises coming from inside — desks banging, feet stamping, children laughing. *Sounds like the teacher's not in there yet . . .* He stood on his tiptoes and peeked in through the window, scanning the crowd for a pair of ginger pigtails. He opened the door just a crack . . .

'What's inside your backpack, then?'

'Me-me-me — I wanna see!'

'Go on, Coco – show us!'

Jack went cold. *I don't believe it. The ginger-crossing, freckle-stabbing, feather-filching traitor.*

SIX

'Everybody, freeze!' yelled Jack. Twenty-seven faces turned and stared. There she was, in the middle of the crowd, with her backpack by her feet. Jack strode forwards, the crowd parted and – *bam!* – he slammed his fist on a desk. 'Okay, Coco – the show's over. Take your hands off the flap and step away from the bag. One false move and you're macaroni cheese.'

'Who's *he*?' said a girl with a big yellow bow in her hair. 'Does anyone know this freak?'

Coco sighed. 'Rubella Sneake – meet

Jack Dash. Don't worry, he can't help it – he just goes a bit weird sometimes.'

Jack looked round at the ring of faces – they were nudging each other and muttering. He pointed to the window with a trembling finger. 'There's – there's a reindeer up in that tree.'

'No way!'

'Really?'

'Lemme see – lemme see – lemme see!'

And twenty-seven children scrambled across the classroom.

'Not so fast.' Jack grabbed Coco's arm and pulled her aside. 'I don't *believe* you,' he rasped. 'Exactly which bit of *don't show anyone* did you not understand?'

'Who gassed your nappy?' said Coco. 'I was only having a bit of fun.'

'*Fun?*' Jack thrust his face into hers. 'It was supposed to be a secret, remember?'

'Where's the reindeer?' somebody called. 'I can't see anything!'

'The new boy's making it up,' said Rubella. 'Told you he was a freak.' She clicked her fingers and pointed at the floor. 'Open the backpack, Spartacus!'

A big boy with a square head and a bent nose stepped forward.

Oh no, thought Jack. *He's pulling back the flap.*

Pablo's beak popped out.

'What's *that*?' said Rubella.

'Er . . .' Jack felt his forehead go sweaty. 'It's a carrot,' he said.

'A carrot?' Rubella snorted. 'What's so special about a carrot?'

'Um . . . it's an antique carrot,' said Jack. 'It's approximately four hundred and seventy-two years old.'

'Eeeurrgh!' Rubella stepped away from the backpack. 'Coco's right – you *are* weird.'

'Teacher's coming!' someone yelled.

Jack bundled the backpack into his arms as everyone scuttled to their seats. *Gotta hide Pablo. Gotta hide Pablo.* He looked left, he looked right. *Aha!* The wastepaper bin – by the door. *Quick, quick, quick – before someone sees.* One last check behind him and Jack slid the penguin out of Coco's backpack. Pablo glared up at him. He hissed like a kettle and stamped his foot.

'*Please* don't let me down,' Jack whispered. And he slammed the bin over Pablo's head.

'Good morning, Neptune Class!' In lurched

the teacher, with a pile of books in his arms. He had a bushy brown beard and wore a large floppy hat, which was bristling with twigs and leaves.

'GOOD MORNING, MR WAYWOOD!'

Clomp - clomp - clomp – Mr Waywood stomped across the room in his hiking boots, a pair of binoculars swinging round his neck and a whistle and a water bottle hanging from his belt. *Clatter-bam-woomph* – he plonked the books on his desk and stroked his beard, his eyes darting from side to side. 'Something's different in here,' he said. 'I can sense it.'

Dubba-dub, dubba-dub, Jack could hear his heart pounding. *Something's different all right – there's a penguin under the bin right behind you.*

Mr Waywood closed his eyes. He sniffed the air. 'Ah, yes!' he said.

Oh no, thought Jack.

Clomp - clomp - clomp – Mr Waywood was walking around the classroom now, looking left . . . looking right . . . breathing slowly. 'I smell the beginning of an adventure,' he whispered. 'It's dark and dangerous in the jungle ... It's been five long days without food.' He cupped his hand to his ear. 'Listen! Can you hear it?'

The whole class leaned forward.

'Huk-huk-huk!' went the bin.

'I'd know it anywhere!' said Mr Waywood. 'The croak of the poison arrow frog.' **Clomp – clomp – clomp** – he stopped beside Jack's desk. His bushy beard was twitching. 'Aha! What have we here?'

Dubba-dub, dubba-dub – I don't believe it! The bin was sliding across the floor. Jack squeaked like a guinea pig. *No, please, no!* Pablo was heading towards him.

'It's a medium-sized mammal of the human variety,' said Mr Waywood. 'Does he talk? Does anyone know where he's from?'

Zigzag, zigzag – off whizzed the bin again, in between the desks.

'Mr Waywood?'

'Yes, Gilbert?'

'The bin's moving.'

'Moving? Really?' Mr Waywood looked at the bin long and hard – it was lingering by the bookshelf. He took a swig from his water bottle and wiped his beard with the back of his hand. 'Keep calm, everybody – stay alert and keep your eyes peeled. If the bin moves again then raise your hand immediately.'

Up went a hand.

'Yes, George?'

'It's moving again.'

Jack let out another squeak.

'Again? Are you sure?' Mr Waywood grabbed his binoculars and clamped them to his eyes. 'No,' he said. 'The bin is definitely stationary.' He turned to the class and rubbed his hands together. 'Right,' he said. 'Time for the register!'

'Huk!'

'Mr Waywood?' A yellow bow was bouncing. Rubella Sneake was waving. 'The bin just coughed!'

'Hmm . . .' said Mr Waywood. 'Could be an infestation of electromagnetic forces.'

'Oh no!' wailed a small boy as he crawled under his desk.

'Nothing to worry about, Timmy

Tremble – I'm going to perform a thorough investigation.' Mr Waywood dropped to his hands and knees and pressed his ear to the floor.

Jack scrunched up his toes and held his breath. *Please, Pablo, please – keep your orange beak shut.*

'*HAAAAARRRK!*'

Mr Waywood sprang to his feet and jammed his whistle to his lips: **PEEP!** He paced to and fro. 'Don't panic, anyone!' **PEEP-PEEP!** 'Keep calm – it's just a few stray particles.' **PEEP-PEEP-PEEEEP!**
DONG!!!!

A shower of plaster fell from the ceiling.

'Goodness me!' said Mr Waywood, dusting down his shoulders. 'Is it time for assembly already? You know the drill, Neptune Class – tuck your chairs in and proceed to the hall in a calm and orderly fashion!'

Everyone stood. Jack watched them surge through the door and down the corridor. He closed his eyes and counted to ten to steady his thumping heart.

SEVEN

'Coco, wait!'

'Not now, you dingbat – it's assembly. Frostbite will kill us if we're late.'

'But what about Pablo? We can't just leave him under a bin. He could do himself an injury.'

'Relax,' said Coco, heading for the door. 'He'll be fine.'

'HAAARRK!' screeched the bin, as it crashed into the nature table.

'Uh-oh.' Jack scurried over to the bin and whisked it off the floor. 'Pablo?'

The penguin fluffed up his feathers and

narrowed his beady eyes.

'I think he's cross with me, Coco. He's acting kind of funny.'

'Hrrf!' Pablo twitched his head. He looked at Jack's shoe and jabbed it with his beak.

'Ow – ouch – ay-ay-ay!' Jack grabbed his foot and hopped after Pablo, who was waddling over to Rubella's desk. *No, no, no* – he was sticking his head inside her bag and – peck-peck-peck – a raspberry yoghurt splattered across the floor.

'Hmm . . .' said Coco. 'I see what you mean. We'd better take him with us. It should be okay if we sneak in at the back.' She poked her head into the corridor. 'Grab him, will you? We've got to go.'

Jack lunged and scooped the penguin into his arms.

'HAAARK!' screeched Pablo, pecking and flapping.

'Wait for me!' Jack yanked his T-shirt over the penguin's head and stumbled down the corridor.

'You're late!' Miss Frostbite folded her arms and tapped her pointed toe.

She was standing on a stage at the end of the hall, with the whole school in front of her – teachers on chairs and children in rows, sitting cross-legged on the floor.

'Keep walking,' hissed Coco. 'And try to act normal.'

Normal? thought Jack. *I've got a psychotic seabird up my shirt — how'm I s'posed to act normal?*

'Miss McBean – I should have guessed.' Miss Frostbite extended a purple fingernail over the front row. 'If you can't tell the time yet, you can go and sit with the babies!' She peered down her nose and frowned. 'And who's that with you?'

Jack staggered forwards, clamping his arms around his bulging T-shirt: a thousand eyes were following him as he walked towards the stage.

'Aaah!' she purred. 'It's the new boy.' She patted the chair on the stage beside her. 'Come and sit up here next to me!'

The ancient steps creaked as Jack climbed on to the rickety platform. He could feel Pablo squirming – he pulled his arms tighter. He looked at the chair.

He looked at his tummy. *Uh-oh — how am I gonna do this?*

TAP-TAP-TAP went Miss Frostbite's toe.

Jack bent over till his forehead touched his knees and lowered his bottom on to the seat. *Ouch!* Pablo's claw was trapped in his waistband. He slid his hand under his T-shirt and tugged at Pablo's leg.

'Now, then, where were we?' Miss Frostbite snapped open her handbag. She pulled out a little blue notebook and flipped through its pages. 'Ah yes. The results of this morning's tooth inspection. Nineteen children lost a tooth at the weekend. You know the rules — bring your tooth-fairy money to reception by tomorrow morning and pop it in an envelope marked *Frostbite.*' With a flick of her finger, she turned the page. 'Leonardo from Moon Class – stand up!' A tiny boy in the third row shuffled to his feet. 'It's been three weeks. Three whole weeks with a wobbly tooth! Not acceptable, Leonardo – I want the money now.' Miss Frostbite sighed. 'Time to get out the toolbox.' She dropped the notebook into her handbag and snapped it shut. 'I'll see you in my office straight after assembly.'

Pablo, please! Jack bit his lip. He twisted sideways and crossed his legs.

'Well, well, well. We seem to have a problem, Jack.' Miss Frostbite was leaning over him now – he could hear the rasp of her breath . . . he could feel the burn of her stare. She uncurled a bony finger and pointed at his ankle. 'Who can tell the new boy what the Frostbite Rule on socks is?'

'Wear them on your head!' shouted Spartacus.

'Shut up, you overgrown toadstool!' **TAP-TAP-TAP** – Miss Frostbite looked around the hall. 'Anyone else?'

'I know, I know!' called Rubella. 'Socks can be any colour as long as it's regulation beige.'

'Correct!' Miss Frostbite laid her hand on Jack's shoulder and lowered her mouth to his ear. 'Did you hear that?' she breathed. 'Reg-u-lay-shun beige! Coloured socks are for clowns and criminals who will never get a job.'

Jack nodded. He squeezed his eyes shut – Pablo was pecking his armpit. Miss Frostbite removed her hand and – *phew!* – he heard her step away.

'Now, I have very exciting news!' she said. 'We're holding our Summer Fair on Wednesday and the Mayor of Curtly Ambrose is coming!'

'Aaaargh!' cried Jack, slapping his T-shirt.

'Yes!' said Miss Frostbite. 'Isn't it thrilling? And who can tell me what mayors wear?'

'Boxing gloves!' shouted Spartacus.

'Oh dear. Spartacus Thump is being silly again. If he opens his mouth one more time I'll have to get out my stapler.' Miss Frostbite smiled. 'The mayor will be wearing a *chain*,' she said. 'A lovely shiny golden chain!'

'Ooooh!' Jack yelped.

'Yes!' she said. 'And Mr Waywood will be running the raffle. I want every single one of you to donate a prize. Bring them in tomorrow – luxury items only, please – I don't want any tat.'

Peek-peek-peek. Jack scrunched up his toes. *I can't hold out much longer,* he thought.

'Miss Frostbite?' A hand was waving and a yellow bow was bouncing. Rubella Sneake leaped to her feet. 'I can run the refreshments stall. I'll bring homemade cupcakes!'

Everyone started 'ooh'ing and 'aah'ing.

'Quiet!' barked Miss Frostbite. Everyone froze. 'Thank you, Rubella. How very thoughtful. Now sit down and stop showing off. This is *my* assembly.'

Rubella sat down. She stared at her lap. The hall was silent.

Jack could feel a claw in his navel and a wing wedged under his arm. *No, no, no!* He held his breath and – *oof!* – Pablo stabbed his ribcage. Jack gasped. He clenched his teeth. He threw back his head and howled like a dingo.

Five hundred mouths dropped open.

'Aaaa-yeeeee!' Jack arched his back and stuffed his hand up his shirt. 'Aaargh! His left leg shot forward. 'Ay-ay-ay!' He was bouncing up and down on his seat.

SNAP! The stage had split. Jack's chair tilted sideways. Miss Frostbite was staring down at him – Jack felt her hand on his knee.

She curled her lip. 'Bye-bye, Jack – it's been a pleasure!'

And – *crack!* – he heard the splintering of wood as the floor gave way beneath him.

EIGHt

What happened? thought Jack. *Where's everyone gone?* Miss Frostbite . . . the children . . . they'd all disappeared. And the dust! It was everywhere – in his ears . . . on his lap . . . all over his trainers.

'Huk,' went his T-shirt. 'Huk-huk-huk.'

'Pablo?' Jack pulled him out and set him on the floor. 'You okay?'

Pablo blinked. He shook himself. One step forwards, two steps back and he shuffled off sideways into the dark.

Slowly, very slowly, Jack eased himself to his feet. **BOOMPH!** – a door banged open – and there stood Coco, cheeks pink and eyes shining.

'I've been looking for you everywhere,' she said. 'One minute you were up there on the stage and next thing – *bam!* – you'd gone.'

Jack looked round and scratched his head. 'I . . . I must've slipped through an invisible portal and entered a parallel universe.'

'It was Frostbite, you clot-brain! She pushed you through the floor and you landed on that stinky old thing.'

Jack gazed at the battered armchair beneath him . . . at the hole in the ceiling . . . then he wrapped his arms around himself and shivered. Cobwebs sagged like old net curtains and a stack of paint pots rose from the floor. 'Where . . . where are we? It's like no one's been here for centuries.'

'Must be some kind of storeroom.' Coco shut the door behind her and wandered over to a shelf. 'This place is amazing – there's so much stuff.' She picked up a pair of black handsets, pulled out an aerial and twisted a dial. 'Hmm – these look interesting.'

'Put them down. They might be dangerous.'

'They're walkie-talkies, you wombat. They're like mobile phones for old people.' She unhooked a key from a row of rusty nails on the wall and squinted at the label. 'Guess what – it says *clock tower.*'

'That's enough,' said Jack. 'I think we should leave. What if someone comes looking for me, Coco? What if Frostbite—'

'Relax,' she said. 'We've got loads of time. Frostbite's gone to her office with Leonardo and they won't be out for *ages.*' She wiped the dust off a grey plastic box. 'D'you reckon this thing works?'

'I dunno,' said Jack. 'What is it?'

'It's a fax machine. It's how they used to

send letters and stuff before they invented email.' Coco flicked a switch and – **BEEP-BEEP-WHIRR!** – it rattled into life. 'I know – let's fax a letter to the staff room. Tell them there's a woolly mammoth on the loose in the playground.'

'I've had it,' said Jack, heading for the door. 'Grab Pablo, will you? We're going.'

Coco peered at the figure hunched in the corner, hissing and twitching his head. 'Looks like he might throw a wobbly. Maybe we should leave him here.'

'Leave him?' Jack swallowed. 'In a storeroom, in a basement, *on his own*?'

Pablo gazed up at him and then he hung his head.

'He'll be fine,' said Coco. 'We'll come

back at lunchtime and check on him – we can bring him some cushions and loads of toys. Make it nice and cosy.'

'Penguins don't do cosy – they're from the Antarctic, you fruitcake.' Jack bit his lip. *Think, think, think!* An idea was creeping into his brain – he looked at Coco's backpack. *Maybe I could use my . . . No*, he thought. *Too dangerous.*

Pablo sniffed. He lifted his wing and buried his head beneath it.

Jack gulped. He thrust out his hand. 'Pass me the feather, Coco.'

'Now you're talking, Jumping J D!' Coco plunged her arm inside her backpack and handed him a pad of paper. 'What are you gonna draw?'

Jack sat in the armchair and balanced the pad on his knee. 'I'm going to recreate Pablo's natural environment. Make him feel at home.'

'Ooh!' squealed Coco. 'Like a great big ocean and loads of icebergs and one of those massive whales?'

'Just give me the feather, will you?' Jack could feel his fingertips tingling as he took it in his hand. It crackled and fizzed and sparkled, sending shadows dancing up the walls.

'Huk-huk!' went Pablo, flapping his dusty wings.

'Everybody, quiet. I gotta get this right – one false move and I could blow up the school.' Jack took a deep breath and flipped over the page. 'Here goes,' he said and pressed the tip to the paper. He drew one ring inside another.

'I don't get it,' said Coco, leaning over his shoulder. 'Why d'you draw a fried egg?'

'It's a paddling pool. And this . . . ' said Jack, with a squiggle-squiggle-squiggle, 'is the water.' He laid the pad on the floor.

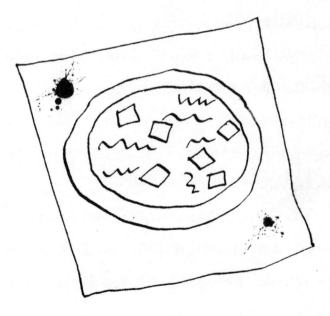

'Hmm . . .' Coco tilted her head. 'What are the blobby bits?'

'Ice cubes, obviously. To replicate the temperature of the Antarctic Ocean.'

'Shame . . .' said Coco. 'Looks like they've already melted.' She twizzled her pigtail and coughed. 'How much longer d'you think it'll take to . . .'

Rattle-rattle-rattle.

Jack froze. 'What was that?' he whispered.

Pablo's eyes widened. He turned his beak to the door.

THUMP-THUMP-THUMP!

'I know you're in there, Coco McBean! You and your freaky friend!'

'Quick,' said Coco. 'It's Rubella!'

Jack stuffed the feather inside her backpack and shoved Pablo under the armchair. 'The paddling pool!' Jack squeaked. 'It'll come to life any second and . . .'

THUMP-THUMP-THUMP!

'Open the door!'

Coco wrenched it open and poked her head outside. 'Oh. It's you. What a lovely surprise.'

'What are you doing in there?' said Rubella, trying to peer over Coco's shoulder. 'You're supposed to be . . .'

DONG!

'Mustn't be late for lessons!' said Coco. She dragged Jack into the corridor and slammed the door behind them.

NINE

Tick-tock, tick-tock.

How much longer? Mr Waywood's been talking for hours. Jack stared at the clock on the classroom wall . . . the dead wasp on the windowsill . . . and back at the clock on the wall. *I wonder what Pablo's up to. He's probably sitting by the pool right now, dipping his toe in the water . . .*

'Right!' said Mr Waywood, rubbing his hands together. 'Can anyone tell me what we get if we cut a circle in half?'

'I know – I know – I know!' Rubella Sneake was waving her hand.

Tick-tock, tick-tock.

I'm gonna draw him a diving board . . . and loads of slides . . . a bumpy one, a twisty one and one with a vertical drop. Jack smiled to himself. *I'm gonna turn the storeroom into a mega-awesome, splash-tastic, penguin-sized water park.*

'Jack?' Mr Waywood was leaning over his desk. 'Any ideas?'

'Um . . .' *What do we get? Think, think, think!* 'Er . . . a pair of headphones?'

'Oh dear.' Mr Waywood peered into his face. 'Pale complexion . . . disordered thoughts . . . the new boy appears confused. Methinks we have another case of electrical interference.'

'Not the magnets again!' wailed Timmy, disappearing under his desk.

'Afraid so,' said Mr Waywood. 'They've followed him around all morning and short-circuited his hippocampus.' He opened a drawer in his desk, grabbed an extendable fishing net and snapped it in place with a *click*. 'Sit tight, Jack — this shouldn't take long.' Mr Waywood turned and waved his hand. 'Clear the immediate area!'

Up jumped Gilbert. Up jumped George. Up jumped Frank and Stella. Frida and Carlo were skipping round the room and Coco was doing a handstand.

Ka-dump! — Mr Waywood leaped on to Jack's desk and wafted the net over his head. 'Don't panic,' he said. 'I'll catch those particles faster than you can say thermonuclear discombobulation!'

Jack froze. A huge figure with a square head was lumbering towards Coco's desk. *Jiggery-pokery – Spartacus Thump's got his hand inside her backpack!* And he was pulling something out. *Breathe, Jack, breathe – remember to breathe!*

Spartacus was holding his feather. He twirled it in his meaty fist and his face stretched into a smirk.

'That's mine!' Jack squawked.

Mr Waywood squinted at his net. 'No,' he said. 'It's definitely mine. I bought it in Kuala Lumpur especially for catching piranhas. Or was it catfish in Mogadishu?'

Splat–splat–splat!– Spartacus Thump was shaking the feather.

'Please,' Jack cried, tugging at Mr

Waywood's sleeve. 'Stop him!'

Mr Waywood swung his net. 'Don't move a muscle – I'll soon have everything tickety-boo!'

Spartacus was scratching his head and giving the feather another shake. **Splat-splat-splat!** There were ants! Everywhere! They were streaming over Coco's desk and pooling on to the floor.

No, no, no. Jack gripped the seat of his chair. *Any second now there'll be scorpions in the bookshelf and tarantulas crawling up the walls!*

Splat-splat-splat! – Spartacus grinned. He tore out a page from Coco's pad and smoothed it on to her desk. He was lowering the nib to the paper.

'Coco! Where are you?' Jack looked

right. He looked left. *I don't believe it!* She was leaning out of the window yelling at passers-by. Jack lurched to his feet and stumbled across the classroom. He snatched up the page with one hand and with the other he reached for his feather. 'You – you lunk-head!' he cried. 'Give it back!'

Whoosh! Down went the net, over Jack's head. He gasped. He spluttered. He felt his face tighten. 'Not so fast,' said Mr Waywood, dragging him back to his seat. 'There's a rather large particle sticking to your forehead.'

Jack fell into his chair with a thump. He stared at the crumpled page in his hand and at the line of ants crawling up his arm.

Gotta get rid of this and fast. He opened his school bag. He fumbled for his lunch box. He stuffed the paper inside it and clicked the lid shut.

DONG!

'Lunch!' yelled Gilbert.

'Lunch!' yelled George.

Through the door they ran – Frank and Stella, Coco, Rubella, Agnes and Martin and Spartacus, still clutching Jack's feather.

Mr Waywood chuckled and folded up his net. 'That could have been distinctly disagreeable,' he said. 'But I think we caught it just in time.'

tEN

'We need to talk . . .' Jack scanned the crowded dining hall. 'In private.' He grabbed Coco's arm and hurried over to an empty table, tucked in the corner at the back.

'Whuzzup?' she said, pulling out a chair. 'You look like Pablo just pooped in your sock.'

'I'll give you a clue.' Jack sat down and plonked his lunch box on the table. 'He's big, he's bad and he's got fists the size of hamburgers.'

'Nope,' said Coco. 'I give up.'

'It's Spartacus Thump, you fruitcake.' Jack checked over his shoulder and leaned across the table. 'He's taken my magic feather. He actually used it. And you were so busy messing about you didn't even notice!'

'Are you *serious*?'

Jack stared at her and nodded. 'What if he uses it again? What if he finds out what it can do, if he hasn't found out already? It'll be a Tyrannosaur-sized disaster! I'm talking tectonic collisions . . . alien invasions . . . intergalactic tsunamis!'

'What are you two whispering about?' Rubella slid her lunch tray on to the table and waved. 'George!' she called. 'Gilbert! Over here – I saved you a place.'

Along came Frida and Carlo and Timmy too.

'I'm starving,' said George, biting into an apple.

'I'm starving,' said Gilbert, biting into an apple.

'Shush!' said Rubella. She pointed at Jack's lunch box. 'What's that noise?' Everyone stopped talking. 'It's coming from in there.' She grabbed it off the table and held it to her ear. 'It's buzzing.' Everyone looked at the lunch box. They looked at Jack and they looked at the lunch box again. 'What d'you keep in here, you freak? A prehistoric parsnip?'

'It's my sandwich,' said Jack. 'Give it back.'

'Take it.' Rubella dropped his lunch box and – **jigga-jigga-jigga** – it skittered across the table, trembling and jittering like an electric toothbrush.

'The magnets!' yelled Timmy, diving under the table.

Jigga-jigga-jigga. Jack grabbed at the lunch box but it sprang from his hand. **Jigga-jigga-jigga** – BANG! Off shot the lid.

'Duck!' yelled Gilbert.

'Duck!' yelled George.

Frida gasped. Carlo screamed.

SPLAT!

Timmy peeped over the edge of the table and gawped at the big yellow bow. 'W-where's Rubella gone? W-what's that stuff all over her head?'

'String!' said Gilbert.

'Worms!' said George.

Plip-plip-plip – down Rubella's face it slid.

'Cool!' said Coco. 'It's like her brain's leaking out of her nostrils.' She plucked a strand from Rubella's ear and wiggled it in the air. 'You'll never guess what – it's spaghetti!'

Jack felt his tummy tighten. *Mum didn't give me spaghetti*. He peeked inside his lunch box – a screwed-up piece of paper . . . a scribble in black ink. He swallowed and slammed the lid shut. *Spartacus . . .*

'Ooh, look,' said Frida. 'Rubella's definitely in there – I can see her nose.'

The tangle of spaghetti slithered on to Rubella's dress and – plop-plop-plop – down to the floor. Her jaw was clenched and her eyes were bulging. She snorted like a warthog and a piece of pasta shot out of her nostril.

'Come on,' said Coco, prodding Jack's arm. 'Time to check on You-Know-Who.'

'Stand back,' said Coco. 'I'm gonna kick the door in.'

'Hold it,' said Jack. 'There's a prestige-edition, penguin-friendly paddling pool in there and it's right behind the—'

BOOMPH! The door slammed open.

'HAAARK!' came a screech from inside.

'Oh, wow!' said Coco. 'You're not gonna believe this.'

'What is it?' said Jack. 'What's happened?' He peered into the dusty gloom. Yes – there was Pablo. He was squatting on a circle in the middle of the floor, staring up at them, feathers bristling.

'I don't get it.' said Jack. 'Where's all the water?' He flicked up the edge of the circle with his toe. 'You've punctured his pool, you fridge magnet! I told you to be careful and now look – it's gone all floppy! It's completely useless!'

Coco giggled.

'It's not funny. How's Pablo s'posed to swim in that thing? How's he gonna practise his high dives?' Jack knelt on the floor and held Pablo's wing. 'Look at him, Coco – he's devastated.'

Coco shrugged. 'He looks okay to me.'

'What's happened to his beak?' Jack peered into Pablo's face and gasped. 'It's bleeding, Coco! The door must've hit it when you kicked it open.'

'It's tomato sauce, you blob-head!'

'This penguin needs specialist attention,' Jack cried. 'He's sustained a serious injury and any second now he could slip into a coma!'

'He's fine. He's been stuffing his face with pizza, that's all.'

'*Pizza?*' Jack stared at Coco and shook his head. 'I dunno what your problem is, but I bet it's hard to spell.'

Coco sighed. 'You didn't draw a paddling pool – you drew a pizza. Family-sized stuffed-crust with extra cheese. I *knew* those ice cubes looked funny.'

'Huk-huk-*heeurggh!*' went Pablo and coughed up a slice of pepperoni.

'I – I don't believe it.' Jack gazed at the mess on the floor. 'Can't I do anything right?'

'Just go easy on the toppings,' said Coco.

'Stick to cheese and tomato next time, okay?'

Jack covered his face with his hands. 'Except there won't be a next time, will there? Cos I don't have my feather any more.'

'It'll be all right,' said Coco. 'We'll get the feather back, I promise.'

'Really?' said Jack. 'How?'

'Easy. I've got a plan.'

Oh great, thought Jack. *A plan from Planet Fruitcake . . . Except she's got us out of trouble before. She sorted out Mayor Gristle.* He opened his fingers a millimetre – Coco was looking at him sideways and twizzling her pigtail. 'Okay,' he said. 'What is it?'

Coco smiled. 'You're going to wrestle Spartacus for it.'

'Huk-huk!' Pablo was flapping his wings.

Jack gawped at her. 'For one crazy millisecond, I thought you said *wrestle Spartacus.*'

'That's right,' said Coco. 'I did.'

'Have you seen the size of him recently?'

'You're a professional, aren't you? Just grab him by his pinkie and flip him on to his back.'

'Hukka–hukka–hukka!' Pablo was plucking at Jack's jeans with his beak. He lifted his foot, crooked his wing and – 'Hoooorrggh!' – he launched himself into the air. Slicing and chopping in a frenzy of feathers, he somersaulted backwards and fell to the floor, where he lay with his beak half-open.

'See?' said Coco. 'It's not that hard.'

'I've . . . er – left my wrestling kit at home,' said Jack. 'How can I wrestle without proper gear?'

'Zero problemo – you can bring it in tomorrow. You'll be awesome!' said Coco, slapping his back. 'Spartacus won't stand a chance.'

ELEVEN

Jack sat up and rubbed his eyes. He'd hardly slept all night. Two words were thudding round his head like bricks in a tumble dryer. Spartacus Thump.

'Dumpling!' His mother was calling up the stairs. 'Breakfast's ready!'

Jack groaned and pulled the duvet over his head. He scrunched his eyes shut. He could feel his chest heaving. *What's the point in breakfast*, he thought, *when it's my last day on the planet?*

'You haven't touched your cereal.' Mrs Dash leaned over the kitchen table. 'Are you all right, Dumpling?'

Jack shook his head. 'I've got bruises all over my thorax and my armpit's covered in scabs, there's a particle sticking to my forehead and everyone thinks I'm a freak.'

'Now, don't be silly,' said his mum. 'I'm sure you'll feel much better once you get to school.'

Yeah right, thought Jack. *Like when Spartacus Thump sits on my head and snaps my patella in half.* He flung back his chair and dropped to his knees. 'Please don't make me go,' he cried, tugging at the hem of Mum's skirt. 'I'll do anything. Anything you say. I'll iron the carpet. I'll hoover my bed. I'll—'

Ding!

'Good grief!' Mr Dash laid his phone on the table and wiped his glasses.

'Lionel?' said Mrs Dash. 'What is it?'

'It's an email . . . from the headmistress . . .' Mr Dash shook his head. 'She's sent us a bill for damage to the school stage.' He looked at Jack and frowned. 'Do you know anything about this?'

'Um . . .'

Cock-a-doodle-doo!

'That's Coco,' said Jack, scrambling to his feet. 'Gotta go.'

'Well?' said Coco. 'Whaddya think?' She nodded at Pablo, who was standing beside her on the doorstep. He was dressed in a brown paper bag and a pair of rubber gloves, with a plastic flowerpot on his head, which had a fluffy green pom-pom stuck to the top.

'Er . . .' Jack stepped back. 'What's he wearing?'

'Swedish national costume, obviously. Oh, we had so much fun getting ready – didn't we, Pablo?'

'Huk-huk!' The paper bag rustled and the green pom-pom bounced.

'Aww, look at him, Jack – it's his first day of school and he's so excited.'

Jack swallowed. 'First day of school? You mean—'

'I've got it all worked out. We're gonna drop him off at the nursery. If anyone asks, just say he's your cousin and he's over here to learn English.'

Jack felt the blood drain from his cheeks and sink to the soles of his trainers. 'Did I just hear that right?'

'Me and Pablo have had a chat. He

says he doesn't like it in the storeroom.'

Pablo was shaking his head.

'He says he gets lonely down there,' said Coco. 'He suffers from mild claustrophobia and he thinks he's allergic to dust.'

Pablo was gazing up at Jack now. He shivered all over and coughed.

'But . . . but the *nursery*?' Jack croaked. 'This is twenty-four-carat craziness, Coco. His name won't be on the register. What's the teacher gonna say?'

'I already thought of that. I've typed up a letter on my dad's computer.'

'And what about the little ones?' said Jack. 'He'll puncture their torsos and peck off their noses. They'll be calling an ambulance before break-time.'

'I've given him a really good talking-to and he's promised he's going to play nicely.' Coco patted Pablo's pom-pom and smiled. 'You'll be as good as gold, won't you, Pablo?'

Pablo nodded. 'Hukka-hukka-hukka!'

'I'm sorry,' said Jack. 'But—'

'Thanks,' said Coco, squeezing Jack's elbow. 'I knew you'd understand.' She looked at Pablo. 'What do you say?'

Pablo shuffled forwards and flung his wings around Jack's leg. 'Huk!' he went. 'Huk-huk-huk!' And he rested his head on Jack's knee.

Ker-chang! – Coco heaved the school gate open. 'Uh-oh.'

Miss Frostbite was standing at the top of the steps again, snatching raffle prizes off the children as they filed past her through the front door.

'Quick,' said Coco. 'You'll have to sneak Pablo round the back.'

'Aren't you coming too? It's his first day – I think he'd like it.'

'Whoopsie! I just remembered – there's a couple of things I've got to do.' Coco shuffled off her backpack and pulled out an envelope. 'Here's the letter. Give it to his teacher. Should do the trick – I signed it from your dad.' She handed Jack a bag of popcorn. 'And don't forget his lunch.'

'You signed it?' said Jack. 'From my dad?'

'Better get a move on.' She nodded at Pablo, who was waddling off with the little ones round the side of the building. Jack scurried after him through a small blue gate, past a slide and a sandpit, and down a path to a shiny red door.

'This is it.' Jack knelt down. He patted Pablo's pom-pom and smoothed out his paper bag. 'There's nothing to worry about,' he said. 'Everyone feels nervous when they start a new school.'

'Huk-huk!'

Jack tucked the bag of popcorn under one of Pablo's gloves and the envelope under the other. 'Be good,' he said.

'Work hard, listen to the teacher and definitely don't poop in the toy box.'

Rustle, rustle, rustle went Pablo's tail.

Jack kissed him on the cheek and stood by the gate, waving as Pablo followed the little ones through the red door. He waited and he waited till he couldn't see Pablo's pom-pom any more.

I better find Coco, Jack thought, *and tell her Pablo's okay.* He turned towards the playground. Over in the corner he could see a crowd – Gilbert and George and Frank and Stella and half the children from Neptune class, laughing and jumping and shouting:

'I can't wait!'

'What time's it starting?'

'How much are the tickets, Coco?'

What's going on? What in the world is The Fruitcake doing? Jack's heart began to thump as he ran across the playground – Coco was handing Frank a piece of paper and rattling a tin.

'Lemme see that!' he said and grabbed it from her hand.

JUMPING JACK
DANJERUS v
SPARTACUS THUMP

IN THE PLAYGROWND
AT BRAKE
ONLY 10P

Jack blinked. He swallowed. He read it again. Gilbert was slapping him on the back and George was giving him the thumbs up.

'Guess what?' said Coco. 'We've almost sold out.'

'Oh no!' cried Jack, clapping his hand to his forehead. 'Can you believe it? I've forgotten my wrestling gear.'

'No probs,' said Coco. 'I brought a spare costume, just in case.' She looked at him and frowned. 'You all right? You've gone yellow again.'

†WELVE

DONG!

'Break-time!' Mr Waywood clapped his hands. 'Everybody out!' he cried. 'Get some fresh air! Inhale the ozone! Oxidise your lungs!'

Jack stood up and stumbled into the corridor. *He's gonna rip my head off. He's gonna squeeze my skull till my eyes pop out and make porridge with my brains.*

'Right,' said Coco. 'I've got your gear.' She rummaged around in her backpack and pulled out a flowery swimsuit. 'I borrowed it off my granny,' she said.

'It might be a teensy bit big but we can tie a knot in the straps.'

'Coco?' croaked Jack. 'About the match. I — I don't think I—'

'Come on, Mr Dangerous — you can't keep your fans waiting.' She pulled him into the playground and pointed to a door by the rubbish bins. 'You'll have to get changed in the boys' toilets.'

'Listen to me, Coco — I— Oof!' Jack went sprawling to the ground. 'What d'you push me for, you ginger-coated maniac? You could've cracked my cranium!'

'Keep down!' Coco hissed, crouching behind a bin. 'It's Spartacus Thump and he's heading this way.'

Bang! – the toilet door slammed.

Coco frowned. 'He's gone inside.' She peeked round the bin again. 'He could be in there for ages – we need a change of plan.' She plunged her arm into her backpack and pulled out a green plastic clothes peg. 'You're going to need this.'

'What for?' said Jack.

'Your nose, of course.' Coco passed him a handle with a fuzzy red ball on the end. 'And you're going to need this too.'

'Yuck,' said Jack. 'What is it?'

'My hairbrush, you dim-bat – it's our secret weapon!'

'You want me to go in there and brush my hair with a clothes peg on my nose while Spartacus Thump is sitting on the toilet?'

'You don't have to go *in* there. You're just going to talk to him, okay?'

'So I'm chatting by the door while he does a Number Two?' Jack shook his head. 'Sorry, Coco. It's not gonna happen.'

'See that?' Coco pointed to a metal pipe jutting from the bottom of the wall. 'It comes out by the basins. I shouted down it once when Timmy Tremble was in there and he stayed off school after that for two whole weeks.' She grabbed the hairbrush and grinned. 'Stand still and open wide – I'm going to disguise your voice.'

Jack crouched on the ground by the open pipe, with the clothes peg pinching his nostrils and the hairbrush handle wedged in his teeth. Coco dragged the rubbish bin over and clambered on to the lid. She raised herself on her tiptoes and peered through a window high up in the wall.

'Perfect,' she whispered, 'he's right by the sinks. Now, repeat after me as loud as you can: *Spartacus Thump, are you there?*'

'Ngharka–ump, gh–uh–nghrr.'

'Hmm . . .' she said. 'Don't think he heard you. Can't you make it a bit more scary? You sound like a homesick hamster.'

'NGHNNNNN,' said Jack. 'NGH–SSSS.'

'Let's swap places. I'm really good at

voices – I was chief pirate in Neptune Class assembly.' Coco jumped down and squatted beside the pipe. Jack climbed on to the bin, the lid wobbling under his trainers. He clutched the windowsill and heaved himself up, as high as he could stretch. He squinted down through the window, on to the top of Spartacus's head.

'**WHOOO-AAAAAAA!**' bellowed Coco and Spartacus jumped like a rabbit.

'**SPARTACUS THUMP – ARE YOU THERE?**'

Spartacus looked down the plughole and scratched his head.

'**I AM THE GHOST OF THE BOYS' BOGS!**'

He bent over and looked under the

basin. He checked behind the taps.

'WHERE IS IT, SPARKY? WHERE'S THE FEATHER?'

He was turning in circles, round and round.

'I CAN'T HEAR YOU, YOU PLOP-HEAD. WHAT HAVE YOU DONE WITH IT?'

A shaky voice drifted up through the pipe. 'I – I gave it to Rubella.'

'THAT STINKY OLD LOUD MOUTH? WHAT D'YOU GIVE IT TO HER FOR?'

'S-swapped it,' he whimpered.

'YOU SWAPPED IT?'

'For a p-packet of crisps and h-half a c-can of cherry Coke.'

I don't believe it! Jack clung to the ledge by his fingernails. *Clatter, clatter, clatter* – the bin lid was wobbling beneath his feet. 'Ngggh–ngggh–aaaagggghhhh!'

Spartacus whirled round and gaped up at the window.

Oh no, oh no, oh no – he's seen me.

The lid slipped away from under him and – *crash!* – Jack tumbled into the bin.

Bang! – the toilet door slammed.

Jack could hear the pounding of feet.

'Ghost!' shouted Spartacus. 'Hairy mouth! Green nose! Horrible!'

tHIRtEEN

'This could be a problem,' said Coco.

'Too right it's a problem,' Jack wailed. 'It's a calamity of catastrophic proportions. Spartacus swapped my feather and he's given it to that—'

'There she is!' Rubella Sneake was pointing straight at them. 'There's Coco McBean!'

'Thank you, Rubella.' Miss Frostbite flick-flicked her hand. 'Now run along, why don't you?' **click-clack, click-clack** – she strutted up to Coco and waved a piece of paper at her. 'Well?' she said. 'Where is it?'

'Where's what?' said Coco.

'Don't *what* me, Miss McBean! You know perfectly well.' Miss Frostbite bent down. Her left nostril quivered. 'You arrange a fight – withoutmypermission! You charge money to watch it – withoutmypermission – and then you pocket the dosh. I'll say it again,' she breathed. 'Where is it? Where's all the money you made?'

Clank! – the nursery gate swung open. *Oh no, oh no, oh no.* A small figure in a brown paper bag and a plastic flowerpot was shuffling across the playground towards them.

Miss Frostbite narrowed her eyes. 'Who or what is *that*?'

'Um . . . he's my cousin,' said Jack. 'He's just started nursery.'

'HAAAARK!' screeched Pablo, gathering speed, his rubber gloves flapping behind him.

No, no, no! Jack leaped forward too late – Pablo lunged at Miss Frostbite's ankle.

'Yeeeee-oooow!' she shrieked. 'What's the matter with the boy?'

'He's Swedish,' said Jack, bundling Pablo into his arms. 'It's – er – how they say hello.'

'Take him away this instant!' spat Miss Frostbite. 'Take him back to the nursery – horrid place for horrid children!' She whirled round to grab Coco's ear. 'We, however, have unfinished business, Miss McBean.'

The clock on the classroom wall was ticking and Mr Waywood was sitting on his desk, with his legs wrapped round the back of his head and his ankles hooked over his ears. He closed his eyes and wiggled his toes. 'Is everybody relaxed?'

Tick-tock, tick-tock.

Nearly lunchtime . . . thought Jack. *Coco's been gone for ages.*

'Take a deep breath,' said Mr Waywood. 'Feel the energy flow to your tonsils . . .'

Tick-tock, tick-tock.

George was sleeping. Gilbert was snoring. Spartacus was picking his nose.

Rubella Sneake was holding a long blue box tied with orange string.

Jack sat up.

She was pulling at the string . . . taking off the lid . . . and her face lit up with a golden glow.

Here's my chance, he thought. *I'll slide across the floor like an anaconda. I'll rear up like a sabre-toothed tiger and snatch it right out of her hands.*

DONG!

Mr Waywood opened his eyes. He unhooked his ankles and brushed the dust off his shoulder. 'Lunchtime!'

Rubella put the lid back on the box and slipped it into her bag.

Clomp – clomp – clomp – Mr

Waywood left the room and the children surged after him into the corridor.

Tick-tock, tick-tock.

The classroom was empty. As Jack pushed back his chair, the door swung open. 'Coco?' She was swaying in the doorway, her pigtails limp and her mouth hanging open. 'What happened?'

She gazed at him with hollow eyes.

'Coco?' He clicked his fingers in her face. 'It's me. Jack.' He grabbed her by the shoulders and shook her. 'Speak to me – *please!*'

Coco's eyelids fluttered. 'Frobbit.'

'Frostbite? She did this to you?'

'Eyes . . . deep . . . blue . . .'

Jack gasped. 'You looked into Frostbite's eyes?'

'Ticket money . . .'

'She took the ticket money?'

Coco nodded. She raised her hand to her jaw and slumped into a chair. 'Toof . . .' she said. 'Wobbly . . . Gone . . .' And she flopped forwards, her forehead slumping down on to the desk.

'Hang in there, Coco. You can get through this. Everything's gonna be okay.' Jack sank to his knees and peered up into her face. 'We'll get my feather back — you'll see. I'll talk it through with Pablo. We'll devise a plan. And then I'll draw you a ton of chocolate and a massive pile of sweets. And . . . and a spacesuit,' he said. 'With a hover board and an oxygen tank and a zero-gravity chamber!' He grasped her hand and joggled her arm. 'Wake up, Coco — *please.*'

FOURTEEN

'I know what you're going to say,' said Mum. 'It won't work, Jack – you're going to school today and—'

'Okay,' said Jack, shovelling cereal into his mouth.

'Your father and I have been talking. And we're not having any more silly nonsense, are we, Lionel?'

'Extraordinary!' Dad stared at his phone. 'It's from the school again.' He shook his head and looked at Jack. 'Something about your Swedish cousin.'

Uh-oh. Jack tipped the bowl to his lips

and slurped up the last of the milk.

Cock-a-doodle-doooo!

'That'll be Coco,' said Mum, handing Jack his school bag. 'I've packed you a tuna and beetroot jelly sandwich and—'

'See you later!' Jack's chair clattered over as he leaped to his feet and – *bang!* – he slammed the kitchen door shut.

'Pablo?' Jack glanced up the stairs – a small dark figure had appeared on the landing. 'You ready?' he whispered.

Pablo nodded and – *bump, scrabble, bump* – he hopped down the steps.

'This is it,' said Jack. 'Operation Golden Retriever.' He knelt down to straighten Pablo's flowerpot and patted him on the wing. 'We're going to get my feather back.'

The Summer Fair was about to start — the children and teachers had set out all the tables. Red and yellow flags were flapping in the breeze. Here were the mums and dads, uncles and aunts, grannies and granddads, brothers and sisters and screaming babies — coming down the steps and into the playground.

'Pay attention, you two,' said Jack. 'We need to stick together.'

'Huk-huk-huk!' went Pablo, jumping up and down.

'This is a multi-mega-dangerous mission,' he said. 'We can't afford to make any mistakes. Are you sure you've completely recovered, Coco?'

'I already told you – I'm fine.'

'I think I'd better double-check,' said Jack, laying his hand on her forehead. 'Have you had any symptoms since yesterday? Dizziness? Double-vision? A tingling sensation in your cerebral cortex?'

'Yester—?' Coco stared out across the playground. Her mouth sagged and her pigtails drooped.

'Coco?' Jack clicked his fingers in her face. 'You okay?'

Coco blinked and shook her head. 'Course I am,' she said, swatting his hand away. 'Come on, Pablo, let's go.'

And Jack scurried after them into the

fair – past Mr Waywood selling raffle tickets from an ice-cream van, Mr Humdrum from Mars Class playing the bagpipes, Miss Index from the library juggling on a unicycle, Miss Rancid from Moon Class painting tiger stripes on a toddler's face. Past the book stall, the tortoise race, past the table with the raffle prizes: bottles of whisky and bars of soap, a silver cake stand and a diving watch, a set of bath towels and a tin of luxury biscuits.

'Behind you,' whispered Coco. 'Yellow bow.'

Jack spun round – over by the treasure map, Rubella Sneake was smoothing a cloth over a table. 'We need to take this slowly,' he said. 'Pick the perfect moment. Take her by surprise.'

They crept a little closer, easing through the crowds. Rubella was unpacking a tub and laying out sandwiches, biscuits and cupcakes, all in perfect rows. Now she was lifting the long blue box tied with orange string.

'I–it's in there!' Jack yelped. 'My feather!'

'Uh-oh,' said Coco. 'She's opening the lid.'

Rubella plucked the feather out – she was tapping the nib with her finger.

'Haark!' squawked Pablo, flapping his gloves.

'Gotta stay calm. Gotta keep cool.' *Bang, bang, bang* – Jack bashed his head with his fist. Now Frank and Stella and Gilbert and George were crowding round and he couldn't see the table any more. 'Coco?' he squealed. 'W–what's going on?'

Coco stood on her tiptoes and craned her neck. 'It's not looking good, Jack – she's got a piece of paper and she's . . .'

'Dumpling!'

No, no, no! Mrs Dash was skipping towards them in a ballet skirt and a lilac tiara. 'Pablo! Coco! *Do* something!'

'Isn't this fun?' Mum clasped her hands together and beamed. 'Your father's having such a lovely time with Miss Snakebite.'

Jack could hear Rubella shouting, 'Get your hands off my poster, Coco McBean!'

'Did you brush your hair this morning?' asked Mum. 'It's looking very untidy.'

'Er . . .' Rubella was stamping her foot and wagging her finger in Coco's face.

Jack's mum pulled a comb from her pocket. 'Come here, sweetie, and let me—'

WHOOMPH! A gust of wind blasted through the playground.

Splat! – Mr Waywood dropped his

ice-cream cone. Miss Index toppled off her unicycle. Mr Humdrum's mouth fell open and his bagpipes wheezed into silence.

'Goodness gracious!' said Mrs Dash. 'What on earth is *that*?'

There was something on the ground ten metres away – something big and yellow and shiny. Frank and Stella and Frida and Carlo and half the children from Moon Class were gathering round to watch.

'It's ginormous!'

'It's squidgy!'

Gilbert and George and Agnes and Martin started clambering up the side.

'Oi!' Rubella snatched up the feather and stomped off after them. 'You haven't paid for the biscuits!'

'Oh, what fun!' said Mum. 'I must get your father – he'll want to play on the squidgy castle.'

Jack watched his mum skip away. *That's not a squidgy castle*, he thought. *It's a cupcake. A big bouncy cupcake with a cherry on top. Rubella's poster has come to life.*

'Jack?'

He could hear Coco calling – she was standing alone by Rubella's table, twizzling her pigtail and biting her lip. He stumbled towards her, shaking his head – gone were the biscuits in neat little rows, the sandwiches wrapped in napkins, the line of cupcakes with lemon butter-cream icing. The biscuits were broken . . . the sandwiches squashed . . . the cupcakes crushed to putty.

'Coco?' he croaked. 'W-what happened?'

Up popped a flowerpot from behind a pile of frilly wrappers, followed by a beak smeared with strawberry jam.

'Huk-huk!' went Pablo, rustling his tail and – *splat!* – he pooped on a cupcake.

'Quick!' said Coco. 'Rubella's coming back.' She yanked up the tablecloth. 'Bung him under here.'

Jack grabbed Pablo and hid him underneath. 'Keep your beak shut,' he whispered and flipped the cloth back down.

'AAAAAAAAARGH!!!!' Rubella Sneake was thundering towards them. 'My cupcakes!' she shrieked. 'My cookies! My . . . my . . . AAAAAAAAARGH!!!!'

Coco grinned. 'Hello, Rubella! Enjoying the fair?'

Rubella stared at the table. Her yellow bow was quivering. 'I'm telling.' She scrunched her face up and squeezed out a tear. 'MISS FRO—'

'Wait!' Coco clamped her hand over Rubella's mouth. 'I'll fix it, okay? Just give me that feather and I'll get you more food.'

'Food?' said Rubella. 'What kind of food?'

'Pizza,' said Coco. 'Family-size stuffed crust with extra cheese.'

Rubella narrowed her eyes. She looked at the feather. 'And extra pepperoni?'

Coco nodded. 'And extra pepperoni.' She reached for the feather.

'Not so fast!' Rubella said, snatching her hand away. She laid the feather in its blue box and tied up the string with a bow. 'Better keep this safe,' she said. 'Until you bring me the pizza.' She slipped the box under the table. 'There!' She smiled at Coco. 'I'll take one hundred. In the next ten minutes. That won't be a problem, will it?'

'One hundred?'

'Let's make that two hundred. Or shall I call Miss Frostbite?'

'It's a deal,' said Coco. 'Two hundred family-size pizzas coming up!'

'How?' said Jack. 'Exactly *how* are you going to get two hundred pizzas, Coco?'

'Easy,' she said, patting her backpack. 'Your drawing of the paddling pool, remember?'

'Great,' said Jack, rolling his eyes. 'We'll just scrape up the bits off the storeroom floor and serve them up to Rubella, shall we? Hey!' he cried. 'Where are you going?'

'To the staff room,' called Coco. 'I'm going to use the photocopier.'

FIFTEEN

'Of all your ginger-brained ideas,' said Jack, 'this is actually one of your worst. What do we do if a teacher turns up?'

'They're all in the playground, you dumb-bell.' Coco opened the staff-room door and strode towards the photocopier, plonked her backpack on the carpet and pulled out the pad of paper. 'Now, where's your drawing of the paddling pool?' She tore out the first page, then the second. 'Aha!'

'And what if the drawing doesn't work?' said Jack. 'What if the magic's used up?'

'We gotta try something,' said Coco and flipped up the photocopier's lid.

'If Frostbite finds out she'll zap us on the spot. She'll chargrill our eyeballs. She'll nuke our optic nerves. She'll—

'D'you want your feather back or don't you?' Coco slammed the drawing on to the glass and tapped in '200' on the keypad. 'Do me a favour? Go and keep a lookout.'

Jack slipped into the corridor and clicked the door shut. Past Moon Class . . . Star Class . . . Sun Class . . . he tiptoed to the end. He looked left. He looked right. *Hurry, Coco – hurry!*

He heard a creak and turned round: the staff-room door was opening.

A ginger pigtail was poking out.

'I think you'd better come back,' said Coco. 'There's been a bit of an incident.'

'Flip my pancake and fold it sideways!' Jack slammed the door shut and reeled backwards. The staff room was teeming with black and white. Penguins were everywhere: on the comfy chairs . . . under the coffee table . . . in the biscuit tin . . . each one busy with its very own act of destruction. 'C-Coco?' he croaked. 'What have you done?'

She held up a piece of paper.

'B-but that's my picture of the paddling

pool . . .' Jack pointed at the photocopier.
'So what did you . . .?'

Coco bit her lip. 'I must've mixed up the
drawings by mistake.'

'You – you mean you copied your
picture of Pablo? And you printed it two

hundred times?' Jack clapped his hand to his forehead. 'Just how stupid are you on a scale of one to two?'

'Hmm . . .' Coco leaned over the photocopier and read the digital display. 'It actually says a hundred and seventeen.' She looked at a white penguin squatting on the fridge. 'I think the photocopier ran out of toner. That's annoying. We won't be able to copy the pizza now.' She frowned at Jack. 'You okay? You're making a funny noise.'

Jack folded his arms and bent over double. 'I – I think my stomach just snapped.'

Peck-peck-peck! He jerked up again – a small team of penguins was jabbing holes in the carpet and three were on a teacher's desk, shredding a pile of homework. The white one waddled past with a chocolate biscuit in its beak and a sticky yellow label stuck to its wing.

Coco beamed. 'You've got to admit they're cutie-pies. One hundred and seventeen Pablos without the orange bits!'

PING! – the computer in the corner started flashing.

'What's going on now?' Jack wailed.

'One of them's sitting on the mouse,' said Coco. 'Probably thinks it's an egg.

'I knew it, I knew it, I knew it!' moaned Jack. 'I knew this was a terrible idea. We gotta get them out of here!'

'Okey-dokey.' Coco opened the door. 'We'll head straight down the corridor and march them through the front entrance.'

'Down the corridor and through the front entrance? And then what, you nut-job? Take them for walkies down the high street?'

Coco shrugged. 'Sounds all right to me.'

'There has to be another way.' *Think, think, think.* Jack pointed to a door in the corner of the staff room. 'What's through there?'

SIXTEEN

'Huk-huk-huk-huk!' Off went the penguins, waddling through the library – poking their beaks in the bookshelves and scuttling under the tables. A pair of penguins scuttled off to look at the picture books.

'Stop them!' Jack yelled.

Honk-honk-honk! In the Early Learning Section two penguins were fighting a tug of war over *The Starving Centipede.*

'Help!' Jack yelled. 'They're ripping it to pieces and one of them's pooped on the reading mat.'

'Listen to this!' Coco was sitting on the floor with the white one on her lap, reading a magazine. 'It says here that penguins can communicate over hundreds of miles. They've got some sort of homing instinct.'

'Thanks for that, Professor Penguin. And does it tell us how we stop them demolishing the library?'

'They're probably hungry,' said Coco. 'It says here they like eating krill.'

'Guess what?' said Jack, patting his pockets. 'I just realised I'm all out of krill.'

'Fine,' said Coco. 'We'll take them to the kitchen – it's right through that door. You lead the way and I'll bring up the rear.'

'Brrrr!' said Coco. 'It's like the South Pole in here – why have you got the freezer door open?'

'It's the only way to calm them down.' Jack closed a box of Crispy Codpieces, popped them on the top shelf and surveyed the huddle of penguins, dozing on the floor by the glow of the freezer. ''S'funny – they don't look so bad when they're asleep.'

Patter-pat-pat – Pablo waddled into the kitchen.

'Ooh,' said Coco. 'Look who's here! And look what he's got in his beak!'

Jack clapped his hands and laughed out loud. 'My feather!'

Pablo looked up at him and waggled his tail, dropped the feather on the floor and – 'Heeeurcch!' – coughed up a bit of blue cardboard and a scrap of orange string.

'Pablo – you're amazing! You're a genius! You're . . . you're . . .' Jack closed his eyes. *At last!* He could hear the hum of the freezer. The snuffle and snore of the penguins. The pulse of his beating heart. *My magic feather's back!* He wiped his cheek with

the back of his hand. 'I − I can't believe it!'
He opened his eyes and looked round the
kitchen. 'Pablo . . .' he said. 'Where's Coco
gone? And where's my magic feather?'

Jack followed Pablo into the library: round
the broken bookshelf lying on its side, past
the shredded magazines and *The Starving
Centipede*, which lay in shreds on the floor,
the white splats of penguin poop trodden
into the carpet. And there was Coco, bent
over a table.

'Hey!' he cried. 'What d'you run off for,
you fruitcake?' He snatched up his feather
from the table, stroking its shimmering

fronds. He held it up to window and it sparkled and crackled like a flame.

'Jack? I need to tell you something. Promise you won't do a weirdy?'

'My feather,' he murmured. 'My magnificent, magical, mind-blowing feather!'

'I – er . . . I used it again,' said Coco.

The feather fell to the library table. Pablo's beak dropped open.

'You *what?*' Jack gawped at her, heat flooding his cheeks.

'Don't get your knickers in a noodle – it was only a couple of splats. In fact, I did us both a favour – they'll have to stop the fair now. We won't have to get the pizzas any more – we can have the afternoon off!'

'What are you on about, Coco? What exactly did you . . . Oh.' On the table lay a photo of Curtly Ambrose school, mounted in a cardboard frame. He picked it up. 'Where'd you get this?'

'Right there – it was on Miss Index's desk.'

Jack took a closer look. 'You . . . you've scribbled all over it.'

'They're only clouds, Jack – it's no big deal.'

Jack studied the inky smudges and streaks . . . the spots and spirals spattered across the sky. 'What's that, then?' he said, pointing to a jagged line above the school roof.

'Oh, yeah – and a teensy zigzag. Practically an accident.'

'It's a lightning bolt and you know it. This is no accident – it's a full-on electrical storm! And there's one *teensy* problem, Coco. We don't know how to make it stop.'

'I could add a bit of wind,' she said. 'Like last time, remember? When we sent Mayor Gristle out to sea in that manky old boat and—'

'Don't even think about it.' Jack snatched up the photo and – **CRACK!** – the sky flashed like a camera and the air trembled with a roll of thunder.

'Brilliant!' said Coco. 'It's starting!' She dragged a couple of chairs to the window and Pablo hopped on to her lap. 'Come and join us, Jack – this is better than watching YouTube.'

Tuppa-tuppa-tuppa – the rain was drumming on the glass. Out in the playground, children and parents were running for cover and clustering under the trees. Miss Frostbite teetered down the steps, holding a silver umbrella. She waved her finger at the raffle prizes and the teachers and Mr Bodger followed, splashing their way through the puddles, scooping the prizes off the table and carrying them into the hall.

The sky split with another **CRACK!** – the windowpanes rattled and an avalanche of tiles smashed to the ground.

'Did you see that?' said Jack. 'If it doesn't stop soon it could blow the whole roof off.'

'Wow.' Coco looked up at the angry clouds gathering in the sky. 'They'll have to shut the school down.'

'Yep,' said Jack. 'We're one teensy millisecond off a full-on, catastrophic, double-dip disaster.'

Coco turned to him and grinned. 'So, what's the problem exactly?'

SEVENTEEN

'It's like a lake out there,' said Jack. The rain was gliding down the panes so fast it was hard to see out any more. 'Everyone's gone inside.'

Huk-huk-huk – Pablo flapped his gloves.

TAP–TAP–TAP – he pecked at the window.

'What is it?' Jack squished his nose to the glass. 'Flaming tonsils – the bouncy cupcake's gone AWOL!' It was floating past the climbing frame – rising and falling and dipping and tilting. 'I don't believe it – there's someone on it!'

'Only me!' Mr Waywood clomped into

the library, waving his fishing net. 'I'm on the hunt for stray particles. Can't be too careful in this weather. Great Scott!' He clamped his binoculars to his face. 'Is that young Timmy Tremble out there?'

CRACK! – the lake shone silver. Yes, it was Timmy. He was clinging to the cherry like a baby orangutan, cringing under the pelting rain.

'Extraordinary,' said Mr Waywood. 'He's riding bareback on the bouncy castle. Braving the elements! Battling the storm like a hero!'

'Can't you swim out and save him?' said Jack.

'Me?' Mr Waywood shook his head and chuckled. 'I can't swim. I'll tell you a little secret,' he said. 'I've never been out of Curtly Ambrose.' He looked up at the sky and stroked his beard. 'Nothing to worry about – it'll soon blow over.' He took a swig of his water bottle and **clomp – clomp – clomp** – Mr Waywood strode out of the library.

Think, think, think! Jack paced to and fro. 'I know!' he said. 'I'll rub the drawing out.' He licked his finger and rubbed the photo. 'No good – it's scratched in too deep.' His eyes darted across the room and settled on Miss Index's desk. *A pencil case.* He ran over and tipped it out. Pencils . . . a sharpener . . . and – 'Yes!' he cried. 'White-Ex.'

'Why what?' said Coco.

'Correction fluid,' said Jack, as he twisted off the cap. 'Sticky white stuff in a bottle with a sponge.'

'Correction fluid? Now that's genius!'

'It better be,' said Jack, his sponge at the ready. **Dab-dab-dab** – he whited out the scribble – every smudge, every streak, every smear.

'The rain's stopping,' said Jack. 'I think the White-Ex worked.' He peered over the lake to the top of the climbing frame. 'It's like the end of the world out there.'

A grey mist hung over the water, winding up through the branches of the trees. The yellow cupcake was bobbing in the haze, with Timmy Tremble still clinging to the cherry.

'What now?' asked Coco.

Pablo shrugged.

'Only one thing for it,' said Jack. He sat down at a table and picked up his feather. 'Pass me the paper, Coco.'

'Yay!' she said. 'What are you gonna draw?'

'It's a rapid-response all-weather speedboat,' said Jack, as he glided the feather tip over the page. 'It's gotta be watertight so I can't leave any gaps.'

'It's a bit flat, isn't it? I thought speedboats were s'posed to have rudders and stuff.'

'It's streamlined, you fruitcake — she'll cut through the waves like a swordfish.' Jack laid the drawing on the table. 'Stand back. She's gonna be a big one!'

ZAP! CLANG!

'HAARK!' shrieked Pablo, staggering back in alarm.

'Nope,' said Coco. 'That's definitely not a speedboat.' She tilted her head.

'It actually looks more like an ironing board.'

'Course it's a speedboat,' said Jack. 'Don't you know *anything* about marine engineering? Just you wait till she hits the water.' He slid the window open and tipped it out nose first.

SPLASH!

They poked their heads out and peered down at the lake – bubbles were frothing on the surface.

'I think it's sinking,' said Coco.

'She's adjusting to the waves, that's all. She'll find her balance soon enough.'

'Thought so,' said Coco. 'It's sunk.'

'Think, think, think!' Jack looked around the library. 'I need to find something that floats.'

'Huk-huk!' Pablo was pecking at a table.

'Quick thinking, Pablo! Over here, Coco,' he called. 'We need to get it out.' With a heave and a grunt, they hoisted it on to the sill. 'Easy does it,' said Jack. 'Tilt her forwards . . . And – *push*!'

SPLASH!

'That was fun!' said Coco, rubbing her hands. 'What shall we chuck out now?'

We need a sail, thought Jack. *Or a pair of oars.* 'Of course!' He wrenched the fire extinguisher from its clip on the wall and clutched it in his arms.

'Yay!' Coco beamed. 'This is gonna make the biggest splash ever!'

'We're not throwing this out – it's our jet-propulsion motor. I'm gonna point the spray at the water and – *whoosh!* – we'll zip across in record time.'

'You don't mean . . .' Coco leaned out of the window and peered at the table listing on the water, its four legs pointing to the sky. 'We're not riding on that thing, are we?'

'That *thing*,' said Jack, 'is an open-access, flat-bottomed sea vessel, ideal for high-risk rescue operations. Who's boarding first?'

'Huk-huk!'

Jack popped Pablo on to the windowsill, took off his flowerpot and peeled off his gloves. 'Be careful,' he said. 'The water's choppy and you'll be out of your depth.'

Pablo nodded. He closed his eyes. He aimed his beak at the lake and raised his wings to the sky. Flexing his knees, he sprang from the ledge – flipping and twisting over and over – a blur of black and white. He pointed his toes as his beak hit the water and – *splash!* – he disappeared. Two point four seconds later and up scrabbled Pablo, on to the table.

'Bagsy I go next!' Coco shuffled off her backpack and dropped it on to the floor. Out of the window she slid, feet first and – *boomph!* – she landed on the vessel.

Jack hefted the fire extinguisher on to the sill. 'Pay attention, Coco – I'm passing the engine down.'

'Aye-aye, Cap'n.'

'I'm warning you, it weighs a ton.' Jack lowered the extinguisher into her outstretched arms. 'You sure you got it?'

'Aye-aye, Cap'n!' said Coco, staggering across the tabletop.

'Keep her steady – I'm coming aboard.' Jack crouched on the sill. Down-up, down-up – the table pitched and rolled.

'Hurry up,' cried Coco. 'It's freezing out here!'

Jack took a deep breath. *One, two, three* – and – *ooof!* – his knees buckled as his

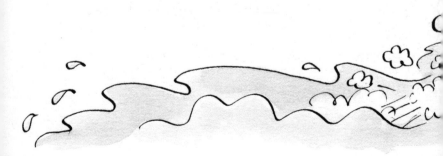

feet hit the wood. Coco passed him the fire extinguisher and he squatted on his heels, gripping it between his knees. He wiped his brow with the back of his hand. 'Ready?'

'Yep,' said Coco.

'Huk-huk!' said Pablo.

Jack pointed the nozzle at the water, clenched his teeth and squeezed the trigger.

EIGHTEEN

Pa-pa-phttt.

'Huh?' Jack held the hose to his ear and gave it a shake. Nothing. He bashed it with his fist – it gurgled and spat. 'I think it's broken.'

'Lemme try,' said Coco. With one massive swipe, she whacked it on the table leg. **WHOOSH!** – out shot the water, up reared the table and back they reeled.

'Ride 'em cowboy!' Coco whooped, punching the air as they bounced and slammed over the waves, a wall of spray on either side.

Through the mist a tall dark shape was looming.

Jack snatched up the nozzle and aimed it at the water. 'I need you to navigate,' he yelled. 'Port's on the left and starboard's on the right.'

'Aye-aye,' said Coco. 'Tree on the starport, Cap'n!'

Jack swung the hose and they veered around its trunk.

'Watch out,' cried Coco. 'It's the ice-cream van!'

'Haaaark!' screeched Pablo, flinging his wings in the air.

Jack yanked the hose back and they swerved past the serving hatch. *Keep her steady*, he told himself. *Nozzle to port, prow to starboard.*

'Timmy on the starside!' hollered Coco.

'You what?'

'The bouncy cupcake, you dung-head – it's back there!'

Jack swivelled the hose one hundred and eighty degrees and they cut through the waves, skimming over the lake in a huge semi-circle. **Jugga-dump-jugga-dump** – the extinguisher was thumping between his knees and the wind was lashing his face. He released the trigger and they shuddered to a halt.

'Hrrrff!' Pablo shook himself all over.

'Wowza,' said Coco. 'That was even better than the Doughnut of Death at Barchester Towers.'

Jack grabbed a table leg and stumbled

to his feet. His cheeks were stinging and his knees were buzzing. He peered through the mist – he could see a large yellow shape behind them, tilting and rocking in their wake.

He cupped his hands to his mouth:'Ahoy there, Timmy – we've come to rescue you!' Silence . . . except for the sound of his own teeth chattering. He glanced at the murky water and shuddered. 'You don't think something's happened to him, do you?'

'Let me try,' said Coco. 'Timmy!' she bawled. 'If you want a lift back then shift your bum.'

'I c-c-can't,' came a distant voice. 'I'm s-s-stuck!'

'Let go of the cherry, you lemming!'

'Never!' Timmy wailed. 'I'll fall!'

Coco shrugged. 'Least we tried. Fire up the motor and let's go for another ride.'

'We can't give up now,' said Jack. 'If he won't come down then we'll have to tow the cupcake back to shore.' He unwound his scarf. 'I'll lasso the cherry with this.' He tied a loop at the end and threw it at the cupcake. **Splosh!**

'It's not long enough, you dilbert.'

Jack leaned over the side of the table – toys and trainers and sponge balls were tangled up like pondweed. He fished out a skipping rope and knotted it to his scarf.

'Here goes.' He whirled the loop over his head, round and round, faster and faster. 'Anchors away!' With a snap of his wrist, the loop sliced through the air and landed round the cherry with a thump. One jerk of his arm and he pulled the rope taut. '*Yesss!* D'you see that? I did it! . . . Coco? . . . Pablo?'

They were both gazing up at the sky.

'Guess what?' Coco grinned, her cheeks pink and eyes shining. 'It's snowing!'

'Of course,' said Jack, as they motored back over the lake – **jugga-dump-jugga-dump** – the fire extinguisher bouncing between his knees. 'How could I be so stupid?'

'You what?' Coco yelled.

Jack stopped the fire extinguisher and

they glided to a halt, the bouncy cupcake bobbing behind them, with Timmy Tremble still clinging to the cherry.

'It's so obvious.' He looked up at the swirling snowflakes. 'I can't believe I only just got it.'

'Got what, Jack? What are you on about?'

'All this,' he said, wafting his arm through the air. 'Don't you see? It's the White-Ex. On the photo. It turned the ink to snow.'

'Hukka-hukka!' Pablo pointed his beak at the clock tower. He fluffed up his feathers and narrowed his eyes. A light was on in the top window and a long lean silhouette was framed in its arch.

Coco shivered. 'It looks just like . . . like . . .'

'What's happening?' wailed Timmy, still clinging to the cupcake. 'What are we stopping for? I'm cold, I'm scared and I want my mummy!'

Jack sat down and squeezed the trigger. 'It won't budge,' he said. 'The mechanism's frozen.'

'Can't you give it a shake or something?' said Coco.

Jack blew on to his hands. 'I'm trying but I can't feel my fingers any more. I'll raise the alarm and hope someone hears.' He stood on his tiptoes. 'HELP!'

Coco shook her head. 'Nada. They've all gone inside.'

'We're adrift in a blizzard on the open seas and we could be stuck here for weeks.' Jack looked up at the bouncy cupcake and gulped. *Timmy's gonna turn into an ice cube up there. We'll have to chip him free.* 'Coco,' he said, 'the situation's reached a critical level. We've got to get Timmy off the bouncy cupcake.' He took a deep breath. 'There's only one thing for it. I'll have to climb up and get him.' He looked up at the shiny yellow wall and swallowed. 'It's actually quite high when you get up close.'

'Just bend your knees and jump,' said Coco.

One, two, three and – *boof!* – Jack hit the side of the cupcake.

'AAARGH!' screamed Timmy.

Jack grasped at the wall but he couldn't get a grip – he could hear the plastic squeaking as he slid down the side. *This is it*, he thought. *They'll have to send in a team of divers to pull my body out of the water.*

Boomph!

'You okay?' said Coco.

'I . . . I think so.' Jack stamped his feet. 'But it looks like we'll have to walk – the water's frozen over.'

NINETEEN

Jack pushed the doors open. The hall was packed – teachers and children, mums and dads, uncles and aunts, grannies and granddads, brothers and sisters and screaming babies. Chairs and prams. Puddles on the floor. **Drip, drip, drip** from the ceiling.

'There's Mummy!' cried Timmy and disappeared into the crowd.

'Okay, Pablo – if anyone asks, I won you on the tombola.' Coco scooped him into her arms and stamped her feet. 'Now, how about we go to the storeroom and I'll draw us a nice warm fire?'

'You? Draw a fire? Have you cracked your skull completely? Hold on,' said Jack. 'Where *is* my feather exactly?'

'In the library, of course.'

'*What*?' Jack stared at her. 'You're joking, right?'

Coco sighed and rolled her eyes. 'Don't do a wonky – it'll be fine.'

'You don't get it, do you? What if someone finds it again? What if—'

PEEP-PEEEEEP! – Mr Waywood was blowing his whistle. A hush fell over the hall. **Clomp – clomp – clomp** – he climbed on to the stage. 'Ladies and gentlemen, friends and mammals – it's time to draw the raffle.' He took a swig from his water bottle and turned to the table beside him. He blinked and fanned himself with his hat. 'Extraordinary,' he muttered and the crowd began to murmur. 'The raffle prizes have disappeared.'

'Disappeared?' said Coco. 'Since when did prizes *disappear*?'

'Forget the prizes, you fruitcake – we've gotta go to the library and . . .'

'Dumpling?'

Not again! Jack's mother was pushing her way towards them, dragging Dad behind her. 'Shift it, Coco! I'll keep my mum talking.'

'There you are, sweetie – I've been looking for you everywhere!'

Jack watched Coco dipping through

the crowd, with Pablo tucked under her arm. *Hurry, hurry, hurry!*

'Your father's acting very strangly.' Mrs Dash looked at her husband and shook her head – he was staring out with hollow eyes, his arms dangling and his mouth hanging open. 'I can't get a word out of him,' she said. 'I hope he hasn't picked up a bug – those squidgy castles can be so unhygienic.'

'Dad?' Jack clicked his fingers in front of his father's face. He jiggled his dad's elbow. 'That's not a bug, Mum – he's been—'

'Where is she?' Jack spun round – Rubella was standing before him, hands on her hips and a face like thunder. 'Where's Coco McBean?' she said. 'And where are my two hundred pizzas?'

'Er . . . she's a bit busy at the moment,' said Jack. 'I think she's sorting out the toppings.'

Rubella folded her arms. 'She's in *so* much trouble. Just you wait till Miss Frostbite finds her.'

'W-what d'you mean?'

'Haven't you heard? Coco trashed the library. She went wild in there. She tore up the books and the magazines and there's white paint all over the carpet.'

'No!' said Jack. 'But that wasn't Coco.'

'Of course it was Coco. Miss Frostbite's got proof – she found her backpack in there.'

Jack opened his mouth. He tried to speak but the words were stuck to his tongue.

'I've never seen Miss Frostbite so angry.' Rubella smiled. 'She'll probably get out her pliers and extract all Coco's teeth!'

Jack's head was humming like a jam jar full of hornets. The room began to spin. *What am I gonna do?* He blundered out of the hall and into the corridor. *Think, think, think! Gotta find Coco. Gotta warn her . . . Gotta . . .*

Frostbite! Jack darted back into the shadows. He could see her at the far end of the corridor – a long lean shape in the dim light, teetering towards him with a suitcase in her hand and Coco's backpack on her shoulder.

Jack pressed his back to the wall. The footsteps stopped. Miss Frostbite lowered the suitcase to the floor. *Dubba-dub, dubba-dub* – Jack could feel his heart thrumming in his throat. *Please, please, please – don't let her see me. Just one look and she'll marmalise my mind. She'll suck out my thoughts like a hoover and throw my brains in the bin.*

Jack caught his breath as she teetered away – Coco's backpack was slipping down her shoulder and the flap was hanging open. He raised himself on to his tiptoes and glimpsed a shimmer of gold.

Frostbite's got my magic feather.

†WEN†Y

Jack scuttled to the end of the corridor. He pulled open the door – Miss Frostbite was climbing a spiral staircase, winding out of sight.

DONG!

Jack reeled backwards – ears pounding, teeth rattling, little bits of brick and plaster bouncing off his shoes. *Of course – we're in the clock tower.*

– he heard her footsteps fading into the darkness above.

She must be at the top by now . . .

The scrape of a key . . . The creak of a door . . .

Jack waited. And he waited. *What's she doing up there?*

Clunk! went the door . . . The scrape of a key . . .

— he heard Frostbite's footsteps coming back down the stairs.

Jack squeezed himself into the corner and squashed his cheek to the wall.

– Frostbite flashed straight past him and down the corridor, her suitcase swinging at her side.

No backpack? She must have locked it in the clock tower. What am I gonna do?

'Jack Dash!'

Huh? That sounds just like Coco. So near . . . So real . . .

'Calling Jack Dash – over and out!'

It can't be Coco. Jack spun round, peering into the dark – a figure with a rounded head and splayed wings was plodding down the corridor towards him.

'Pablo?'

The figure looked up at Jack and waggled its tail. 'Jack?'

'I don't believe it – you can *talk*?' Jack knelt down and, taking him by the tip of his wing, looked deep into his eyes. 'Speak to me, Pablo!'

Pszzzztchh . . . A weird hissing noise was coming from Pablo's back. There was something strapped to it – something the size of … *Aha!* – a walkie-talkie – crackling and fizzing as he pressed it to his ear.

'Hello?'

'Where've you been, you wombat? I've been shouting your name for ages.'

'*Coco?*' spluttered Jack. 'Where are you?'

'In the storeroom. We've got a problem. I went to the library but …' **Pszzzztchh** …

'It's too late,' said Jack. 'Frostbite got there first! She found your backpack and she's locked it in the clock tower. She's looking for you, Coco – and she's furious. Fasten your mouth up! Barricade your teeth! Whatever you do, don't leave that room!' **Pszzzztchh** … He tapped the aerial and turned a dial. 'Coco? … Coco? You still there?'

'I'm here, Jack. And I've got a plan . . .'

Oh, here we go.

'Put your hand under Pablo's . . .'

Pszzzztchh . . .

'You must be joking.'

'His beak, Jack – hurry!'

Jack knelt down and put out his hand. Pablo thrust his head forward. He opened his beak and squeezed his eyes tight. 'Huk-huk-*heeeeurrrrrrgh!*' A string of drool dropped on to Jack's finger and something flat and shiny fell into his palm.

'Eeurgh,' said Jack. 'What is it?'

'It's the key for the clock tower, you wing-nut.' **Pszzzztchh** . . .

Up the spiral steps they crept, Jack on tiptoe and Pablo beside him – hop, scrabble, hop – until they reached the top of the clock tower. Jack looked at the key in the palm of his hand and then at the old wooden door . . . at the sign of a skull and cross bones with *KEEP OUT* written underneath. His tummy started churning like a washing machine.

'Maybe we should come back later.'

Pablo shook his head.

'But . . . but I don't think I can do this.'

'Huk-huk!' went Pablo and nudged him with his wing.

Jack nodded. He breathed in deep. 'You're right,' he said. 'I'm Jumping Jack Dangerous. I can do anything.' He slotted the key in the lock and turned it with a clunk. He twisted the handle and pushed at the door. He shoved it with his shoulder. *Think, Jack, think! – how does Coco do it?* One tremendous kick and – *boomph!* – he tumbled into the room.

'Great lolloping ring-tailed lemurs!' Jack sat up – a huge chandelier hung from the ceiling, dripping with a thousand crystals. Heaped on the thick red carpet were boxes and bottles and fancy gifts – a set of bath towels tied with a satin bow . . . a bottle of Loch Manure whisky . . . a tin of all-butter Balmoral shortbread biscuits and a two-tier box of after-dinner chocolate mint thins. 'The raffle prizes,' he murmured. 'Frostbite *stole* the raffle prizes!' In the corner was a big desk with a computer and a printer and a swivel chair. 'And she's stashed them all away in a secret office.'

Jack scrambled to his feet and pushed the door shut. 'Okay, Pablo – we need to be quick. Let's find Coco's backpack and go.' He shook out the towels. He flipped up a cushion. He stumbled over the shortbread tin, scattering biscuits over the floor.

'Huk!'

'Not now, Pablo – can't you see I'm busy?'

'Huk-huk-huk!' Pablo cocked his head and flapped his wings.

'Just hold on, will you? I need to find that backpack.'

Peck-peck-peck – on the door.

'Okay, okay – I'm coming!' Jack picked his way across the room. He eased it open and peeked through the crack. 'There's nothing there, you nincompoop – you must be hearing things.'

Pablo shuffled on to the landing and peered down the stairs. 'KA-KA-KAAAA!'

The tower erupted with screeches and squeals and squawks and hoots as forty . . . fifty . . . sixty . . . penguins scrambled up the steps.

'Stop!' cried Jack. 'You can't come in here!'

One by one the penguins filed past him, hissing and flapping and jostling through the doorway. They clustered around the fancy gifts, squatting on the bath towels and peck-peck-pecking at the all-butter Balmoral shortbread biscuits. Eighty . . . ninety . . . one hundred penguins . . . The

white one shuffled by with a bracelet round
his neck and a diving watch in his beak.

Pszzzztchh . . . 'Calling Jack Dash!'

Jack pressed the walkie-talkie to his ear.
'Coco?'

'Did you find my backpack or what?'

'It's impossible,' he wailed. 'I don't know where to start – there are penguins everywhere and they're trashing all the stuff!'

'Stuff?' **Pszzzztchh** . . . 'What kind of stuff?'

'Bottles and biscuits and fancy gifts – and one of them's pooping on the cake stand.'

'The raffle prizes – I knew it!'

Peck, peck, peck – a penguin was attacking the stapler on Miss Frostbite's desk and another one was squatting on the printer. 'What are you *doing*? Get down!' Jack lurched across the room, waving his arms. 'I don't believe it – there's more!'

Cheque books and credit cards. Coins spilling out of plastic bags, labelled: Tooth

Fairy . . . Late Fines . . . Wrestling Match. A passport and a ticket for Paradise Airlines . . . a jam jar filled with teeth. *She must've been stealing for years*, he thought. *And now she's planning her getaway.*

Pszzzztchh . . . 'Get it out of there now – all of it. It's evidence, Jack! Frostbite's a thief and we can prove it. Just think, we can wake up tomorrow morning and wear any colour socks we like.'

He gazed at the floor and shook his head. 'How? There's a massive pile of it, Coco – higher than Mount Kilimanjaro.'

'Don't worry,' she said. 'I've got a—'

'Hey,' Jack yelped. 'I've found it!' He grabbed Coco's backpack off the chair, pulled up the flap and plunged in his arm.

He dug out a plastic tulip . . . a slice of toast . . . her granny's flowery swimming costume. *It's gotta be in here somewhere.* An apple core . . . a blue plastic bag . . . and – yes! – a glimpse of gold. Shimmering. Sparkling. It fell through his fingers and landed on the desk with a *clunk*.

Dad's chain.

Jack tipped up the backpack. He shook it out. Empty. Nothing. He sank to the floor. *The feather's not in there*, he murmured. *It was Dad's gold chain all along.*

Jack closed his eyes and curled his arms around his knees. There were penguins all around him, squawking and shuffling and pecking and flapping. As he rocked to and fro, he could hear himself moaning.

TWENTY-ONE

Jack reached for his walkie-talkie and clamped it to his ear. 'I . . . I found your backpack, Coco . . .' He swallowed and closed his eyes. 'B–but the feather isn't in it.'

Pszzzztchh . . . 'I know that, you doorknob. I've got it.'

'That's so funny I forgot to laugh.'

'I'm not joking,' she said. 'It's here in the storeroom. **Pszzzztchh** . . . 'Hope you don't mind – I got a bit hungry so I drew myself a meal deal.'

Jack opened his mouth. He couldn't breathe. He clasped his hand to his chest.

Pszzzztchh . . . 'Jack?' she said. 'You still there?'

'But . . . but Frostbite took your backpack,' he said. 'I saw her!'

'The feather wasn't in my backpack, you blob-fish . . .' **Pszzzztchh** . . . 'It was on the library table where you left it.'

Jack blinked. 'On the library table?' He turned to Pablo. 'Is . . . is this true?'

Pablo nodded slowly.

'But . . . but I just risked my life . . .' Jack croaked. 'I followed Frostbite to the clock tower. I got penguin dribble all over my hand!'

'It's not all bad,' said Coco. 'Least you found my backpack.' **Pszzzztchh** . . . 'Listen, Jack – I'm sending you a fax.'

'You're sending me a *fax*? I'm stuck up here with a hundred and seventeen penguins who are trashing the prizes that Frostbite stole and any minute now she could—' **BEEP-BEEP-WHIRR** – the fax machine on Miss Frostbite's desk rattled into life. 'Are you listening to me, Coco? Will you stop messing about with that stupid machine?'

Pszzzztchh . . . 'It's a picture, Jack – and I drew it with the feather. Should print out in a minute – then chuck it out of the window, okay?'

'*Chuck it out of the window?* But . . . but . . .'

The walkie-talkie sputtered and hissed. **Rattle-rattle-rattle! Thump-thump-**

thump! Jack could hear Rubella shouting, 'I know you're in there, Coco McBean!'

'Coco?' he squeaked. 'What's going on?'

THUMP-THUMP-THUMP!

'Open the door,' yelled Rubella, 'or I'm getting Miss Frostbite!'

'Coco? . . . *Coco?*' Jack looked at the walkie-talkie. He tapped it. He shook it. He banged it on his knee.

Pszzzztchh . . .

Come on, come on, come on! Jack drummed his fingers. He prodded the fax – *beep-beep-beep!* – a green light started flashing.

'Huk-huk!'

'Just hang on, Pablo.'

Millimetre by millimetre, Coco's drawing slid on to the tray.

'HAARK!' Pablo was standing by the door, eyes wide and feathers bristling.

'What is it? What's the matter?' Jack wound his way across the room. He pulled the door open and stepped on to the landing.

Every hair on Jack's body stiffened. He felt his mouth go dry. He spun on his heel and slammed back into the office. 'She's coming – she's coming – she's coming! What am I gonna do?' *Think, think, think!* 'Of course! I'll lock us in.' He checked the keyhole. He looked at the floor. 'The key, Pablo – help me find the key!'

Pablo stared at him and gulped.

'Where's the key?' said Jack. 'What have you done with it, Pablo?'

Pablo looked at his tummy and shuffled his orange feet.

'You swallowed it?'

Pablo lifted his wing and buried his head beneath it.

'Right,' said Jack. 'Keep calm. Don't

panic. We gotta hide the penguins. Where? Where? Where?' *The cupboard behind the desk!* Jack flew across the room – penguins scattering left and right – and wrenched it open. 'Help me, Pablo – she'll be here any moment!'

Pablo threw back his head. 'KA–KA KAAAA!' And one hundred and seventeen penguins lifted their heads. They hopped off the bath towels. They jumped off the desk. They shuffled out from under the cushions and waddled into the cupboard. Pecking and flapping, squawking and clawing, Jack scooped them up by the armful and bundled them on to the shelves.

'Okay, you lot. Don't make a sound.'

BEEP-BEEP-BEEP went the printer.

Coco's drawing! What did she say? Jack lunged for the paper and snatched it off the tray. *Chuck it out of the window. Chuck it out of the window.* He flung the window open and threw it into the whirling snow.

tWENtY-tWO

A rattle … a clink … the scrape of a key …

Jack scooped up Pablo and ducked under Miss Frostbite's desk, pulling his knees in as tight as they'd go. *Dubba-dub, dubba-dub* — his heart was thumping and the back of his neck prickled with sweat. *Stay calm. Just keep quiet and she'll go away.*

Clatter-clink-clank.

What was that? Jack held his breath and screwed his eyes shut. *Please, please, please — make her go away. I'll eat my Brussel sprouts and I'll wash my neck and I'll never stuff my dirty socks down the back of the fridge again.*

'Well, well, well. If it isn't the new boy!' Five icy fingers seized him by the arm. Jack tried to wrench free it but the fingers tightened their grip. 'Jack Alphonse Exeter Dash – spying, if I'm not mistaken.'

'Let me go, you thief! You fiend! You . . . You *terrapin*!'

'So you've discovered my secret, have you?' said Miss Frostbite, hauling him on to his feet. She swept her hand around the office. 'Yes – I stole the raffle prizes. I stole the lot!' She snatched up the mayor's chain from her desk and wound it through her fingers. 'And this . . .' she purred. 'The best prize of all!'

Clutching the chain in her purple talons, Miss Frostbite nuzzled it to her cheek. She kissed it. She licked it. She slipped it over her head and smoothed it on to her shoulders. 'Bless your daddy's little beige socks – I took his precious chain and he didn't even notice. He looked into my eyes and went out like a light!'

Miss Frostbite threw back her head and laughed. A chill crept through Jack's bones. *That screech.* It tore through his skull like a high-speed train and sent his hair electric. *It was you*, he thought. *You were in my dream.*

'You won't get away with this,' Jack cried. 'They'll send you to prison and swallow the key!'

'Oh, really?' With a tweak of Jack's ear, Miss Frostbite tugged him to his feet. Her nostrils quivered. Her lips were turning blue. 'And who's going to tell them?'

'I . . . I will.'

'No, you won't, you snivelling smear of snot. And can you tell me why?'

'Ow!' he squeaked.

'Because children who go into the clock tower never come out again.' Miss Frostbite tugged him closer and stared into his face. 'Look at me,' she breathed. 'Look into my eyes!'

This is it, Jack thought, *she's gonna zap me too.*

The room was fading . . . the edges going blurry . . . Her eyes . . . her eyes . . . so big, so shiny, so blue . . .

Jack squirmed himself free, stumbling

backwards and – *oof!* – he sprawled across the floor. He rolled on to his tummy. He began crawling for the door.

'I've locked it, you face-wipe. There's nowhere to crawl.' Miss Frostbite seized Jack by the ankle, dragging him backwards over the carpet. 'Now, do what I tell you and—'

'HAAAAARK!' Pablo shot out from under the desk, scrabbling over the towels as fast as his feet would paddle. Miss Frostbite screamed as he lunged at her kneecap.

'Pablo – no!' Jack yelled. 'Keep away!'

'Hi-*yaaah*!' She kicked out like a kung-fu master, clipping Pablo's wing with her pointed shoe. He spun through the air and landed on the cushion with a – *boomph!*

'You – you grim-face google-eyed

gargoyle!' Jack cried. 'If you've hurt one feather on that penguin's head, I'll— Aaargh!' He could feel Miss Frostbite's fingernails at his collar.

'What will you do, Jack? Run and tell Daddy? He's in La-La Land, remember?' Jack grasped the lid of the biscuit tin as she wrenched him to his knees. Her lip curled. 'Right,' she said. 'Where were we?' She twisted Jack's collar and pulled him closer. Her eyes . . . her eyes . . . so big, so shiny, so blue . . .

With a trembling hand, Jack lifted the biscuit tin lid to shield himself, blocking her zombie stare. He felt his collar loosen. Miss Frostbite's fingers slipped. She staggered back on her spiky heels. She swayed for a moment and slumped to the floor, legs splayed and tongue lolling.

W-what happened? Jack turned the tin lid over and looked at his face in the shiny metal. *Frostbite zapped herself!*

'Pablo? Did you see that?' Jack dropped the lid with a clatter and stumbled across the room. 'Everything's gonna be okay,' he said. 'You can get up now. It's over!' Jack knelt down beside him. 'Come on, Pablo – open your eyes.' He prodded his round white tummy. He jiggled his orange foot. He lifted Pablo's head in his hands and stroked his feathery cheek. 'W-what's she done to you?' he croaked. 'Wake up, Pablo – *please*!' A single tear slipped off the tip of his nose and splashed on to Pablo's wing.

'Hrrghff!' Pablo sat up. He blinked and waggled his head. 'Hrrrrrrghff!'

'Pablo! I thought . . . I thought you were . . . I thought Frostbite had . . . What was that?' Jack turned to where Miss Frostbite lay and − yes! − he heard her moan. 'Uh-oh! This is mega-big-time serious. We gotta get out of here before she comes round.' Jack thrust out his hand. 'I need the key, Pablo. D'you think you can do it?'

Pablo looked up at him. He twitched his head.

'Please, Pablo − concentrate! She could wake up any minute and—'

'Huk-huk!' Pablo hopped off the cushion and pointed his beak at the window. 'Hukka-hukka-hukka!'

Jack squinted into the falling snow. Something was moving far below. Something huge. Something round. He pushed the window open wide and wrapped his scarf tightly around his neck. It was so close he could almost touch it – curved like a dome, with blue and green stripes. Slowly, slowly, it lifted into the air. Higher and higher, the room growing dark as it filled the window.

'Coco's drawing . . .'

Up it rose – up, up, up – a balloon with a basket hanging beneath it. Jack snatched up the bottle of Loch Manure whisky and dumped it in the basket with a clank. He threw in a clock and a fondue set, gardening gloves, aftershave and sandalwood soap, a scented candle, a butterfly brooch, the box of after-dinner mints and the silver-plated teapot.

'Come on!' Jack scooped Pablo into his arms. 'Before we miss our flight.'

DONG!

It hit him like a dumper truck, shockwaves rippling up his spine and juddering through his jaw. His brain was bouncing round his skull and he crumpled to the floor. The chandelier swayed and jangled above him, showering the carpet with crystal beads.

Miss Frostbite sat up. 'Prizes!' she yelled. 'Rich!'

She hauled herself to her feet and weaved her way through the boxes and bottles, a string of dribble swinging from her chin. She stumbled over the cake stand and tottered to her desk. She snatched up the plane ticket, the passport and the coins and crammed them into her pockets.

Oh no, oh no, oh no, thought Jack. *She's heading for the cupboard.*

'Haark!' Pablo buried his face in Jack's shoulder.

Miss Frostbite wrapped her fingers around the handle and yanked it open. 'Magpies . . .' she slurred. 'In my fridge!' She hoiked off her shoe and – *BAM!* – she slammed it on the shelf.

'Nasty!' she yelled.

BAM!

'Dirty!'

BAM!

'Filthy!'

BAM!

Flapping and squawking, the penguins tumbled on to her head – clawing at her shoulders and pooping in her hair.

'Get off me!' cried Miss Frostbite. 'Get off me! Get off me, you vermin!' She wrenched the white one from her face and scrambled on to her chair. They were pecking her kneecaps and snapping at her shins. She hitched her skirt up over her knees and clambered on to her desk.

She's cornered. Jack lurched to his feet. *I'll stun her with this.* He snatched up a cushion and hurled it across the room. *Boomf!* – it bounced off her forehead and hit the wall, banknotes bursting into the air.

'Butterflies!' shrieked Miss Frostbite, as they fluttered all around her. She caught one in her bony fingers and crushed it in her fist. She gazed at the window and curled her lip. 'Balloon . . .'

No, no, no. She was reaching for the chandelier. It creaked and rattled as she heaved it towards her. Miss Frostbite kicked off from the desktop and – 'Wheeeeeeeee!' – she swung out over the office. Jack ducked. The penguins scattered. He heard a pop and a crackle and then the lights went out.

c-c-c-c-**rash!**

A hundred thousand crystal beads hit him like hailstones – clattering on his head and the back of his neck – bouncing off the penguins, pinging off the walls. Beside him on the carpet lay the remains of the chandelier.

Miss Frostbite was standing on the

window ledge, her hair stiff with penguin poop and her suit smeared with slime. 'Now, then,' she said, 'have I got everything?' She patted her pockets and stroked the mayor's chain. 'Splendid!'

She leaned through the window and grabbed a rope, swung her legs over and slipped into the basket.

tWENtY-tHREE

'She's done it, Pablo . . . She's gone.'

Jack stood at the open window and watched the balloon drifting away from him over the frozen playground, through the falling snow. Miss Frostbite was in the basket. He could see her purple talons gripping the rim, the flash of her teeth, the glint of the gold chain. And far below he could see a figure. A figure with pigtails, running and jumping and waving at the balloon.

Pszzzztchh . . . 'Calling Jack Dash! Calling Jack Dash! You did it,' said Coco. 'I can see you!'

Jack picked up his walkie-talkie from

the floor. 'I'm still in the clock tower, you fruitcake.'

He watched her turn towards him. **Pszzzztchh** . . . 'What are you doing up there?' she said. 'What's happened to all the prizes and stuff?'

'Frostbite's got them. She hijacked the balloon.'

'She *what?*' **Pszzzztchh** . . . 'You're not gonna let her get away with this, are you?'

'I'm locked in,' Jack wailed. 'What am I s'posed to do?'

Pszzzztchh . . . 'Pop the balloon, you plop-head!'

Pop the balloon? Pop the balloon? How'm I gonna pop the balloon? Jack's eyes darted round the office. *Think, think, think!*

Pablo was scrabbling over the crystal beads with Miss Frostbite's shoe in his beak. He dropped it beside Jack's trainer and nudged him with his wing. 'Huk-huk!'

'D'you know something, Pablo? It might just work.' Jack snatched up the shoe and tapped its spiky toe. He looked out of the window – the balloon was hovering twenty metres out, high above the climbing frame. 'It's too far to throw – I'm gonna need a catapult.'

He grabbed Miss Frostbite's chair and flipped it on to her desk. *Hmm*, he thought, *I need something stretchy* . . . He snatched up the flowery swimming costume and knotted it to the chair legs. He pulled it back – back, back, back – till he couldn't pull any more. He hooked the heel of the shoe over the swimsuit's strap and pointed the toe at the window. He waited and waited, till the balloon was hanging over the bouncy cupcake.

'Bye-bye, Frostbite!' he murmured and – *twang!* – the shoe shot across the office, through the window and into the sky. *Yes, yes, yes!* – it was arcing through the air and – *no, no, no!* – it was plummeting to the ground.

Pszzzztchh . . . 'Useless,' said the walkie-talkie. 'Hurry up – she's floating away!'

'I've run out of missiles,' Jack cried. 'I need something heavy. I need something sharp. I need— Ouch!' Jack looked down at Pablo and rubbed his ankle. 'What d'you do that for?'

'Huk-huk!' Pablo was running in circles around Jack's feet. 'Hukka-hukka-hukka!' He was hopping up and down. He looked at the balloon. He looked at the catapult. He looked up at Jack – his eyes were shining.

'Oh no,' said Jack. 'You can't be serious.'

Pablo honked. He flapped his wings.

'You mean . . .?' Jack stared at him and shook his head. 'You mean *you* want to pop the balloon?'

Pablo nodded. 'Hukka-hukka-hukka!'

'Read my lips, you black-and-white basket case. Absolutely no flipping way.'

Pablo glared and stamped his foot, his feathers bristling like a toilet brush.

'Forget it,' said Jack. 'You can sulk all

you want – I'm not firing you out of that window.'

Jack picked up the plastic bag and slipped Pablo's wings through the handles. 'And this is your parachute,' he said, tucking the bag under Pablo's wing. 'Remember. This bit's important – release the bag when you burst the balloon.'

'Huk!'

'And you gotta get the landing right. Bend your knees and roll when you hit the ground, okay?'

'Huk-huk!'

Jack lifted Pablo on to Miss Frostbite's desk and stretched the swimming costume under his feet. 'Are you absolutely sure about this?'

Pablo turned his beak to the window – he narrowed his eyes and hissed.

'Ready …' Jack pulled back the costume as far as it would go. 'Aim …'

Pablo flattened his wings by his sides and thrust his orange beak forward.

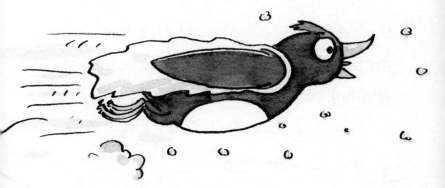

'Fire!' Jack cried and — *snap!* — *TWANG!* — Pablo shot out like a black-and-white torpedo, through the window and into the sky. Jack felt his heart flutter and lurch. *I can't look. I can't look — I can't look — I can't . . .*

BANG! Phhhhhhhhhhht!

'AAAAARGHH!' Jack could hear Miss Frostbite shouting.

'Yes-yes-yessss!' yelled the walkie-talkie.

The balloon was whizzing and twisting through the air, Miss Frostbite clinging to the basket. And all around him on the floor, the penguins were squawking and flapping and hopping.

Uh-oh, thought Jack. *Where's Pablo?*

Round and round, faster and faster,

the balloon spiralled and looped, swinging the basket into the sky and flinging Miss Frostbite free.

'AAAAARGHH!' she screamed, hurtling earthwards. And – *BOING!* – she hit the bouncy cupcake, flip-flopped into the air again and disappeared into the tree.

Jack thrust his head into the blizzard. He clutched at the windowsill, his knuckles turning white. 'Pablo!' he yelled. 'Where are you?'

The penguins were crowding around his feet, staring up at him, their beaks hanging open. Jack clamped his hand to his mouth. He swallowed and closed his eyes. 'W-what have I done?'

'Hukka-hukka-hukka!' The white one

pecked Jack's leg and pointed his beak at the window. And then he saw it – a flash of blue plastic falling through the snow.

'Bend your knees!' Jack yelled. 'Remember to bend your knees!'

He could see Coco skidding across the playground. Then he saw a puff of white as Pablo hit the ground.

Pszzzztchh . . . 'He's coughed up the key,' said the walkie-talkie. 'I'm coming to get you, Jack!'

tWENtY-FOUR

'Oh, Lionel!' Mrs Dash clapped her hands and giggled. 'Aren't they adorable?'

Sixty . . . seventy . . . eighty penguins came through the doors of the hall and into the playground, skidding down the steps with a **bump-bump-bump** and sliding over the snow on their tummies. 'And look! Is that . . . ?' she pointed into the tree and tugged at her husband's elbow. 'Yes!' she said. 'It's your chain!'

'Let me down!' came a shout from somewhere inside the foliage.

Jack's dad reached up and shook a

branch. The leaves rustled. Coins cascaded through the branches and – plop-plop-plop – they landed in the snow. Notes and cheques swirled into the air. And down tumbled the chain, into his hands.

'Get your filthy hands off that!' screeched the voice. 'It's mine!'

The children ran outside, laughing and shouting. Spartacus was hurling snowballs, Agnes and Martin were sledging on a tray, Mr Humdrum was playing the bagpipes

and Miss Index was building an igloo. **Crunch - crunch - crunch** – Mr Waywood strode across the playground in a penguin suit, with a shovel slung over his shoulder and icicles clinging to his beard.

'Hey, Pablo!' Jack waved his arms in the air. 'We're over here!'

A squeal echoed round the playground. Pablo came hurtling over the snow towards them and – *boompf!* – Jack toppled on to the ground.

'Hukka-hukka-hukka!' Pablo was bouncing up and down, flapping and squawking and waggling his tail. He flung his wings around Jack's neck and pecked him on the earlobe.

'You did it!' said Jack. 'You were amazing, Pablo – you popped that balloon like a pro!'

DONG!

Coco shuffled off her backpack, dumped it on the ground and rubbed her palms together. 'Okay, you two – how about one last drawing before we go home?' She plunged in her arm and pulled out Jack's feather. 'I know – let's draw a ski jump off the roof.'

'Hang on,' said Jack, grabbing her hand.

Coco stared at him. 'What d'you mean, *hang on?*'

'We can't leave the weather like this,' he said. 'We can't let it keep on snowing forever.'

Coco shrugged. 'Don't see why not.'

'Just take a look around you,' said Jack. The snow lay on the ground like a thick white duvet, sloping up the walls as far as the windows, and still it kept on falling.

Mr Humdrum was packing up his bagpipes now and Mr Waywood was digging out his van. 'We've started an ice age, Coco. Hedgehogs will go into hibernation. There'll be herds of yetis on the high street.'

'Ooh!' said Coco, clapping her hands. 'I love yetis!'

'And what happens when we run out of food? We'll have to eat ice cubes and slug blubber.' Jack looked up through the swirling snow and gulped. 'We may never see the sun again.'

'Really?' said Coco, twizzling her pigtail. Her face split into a smile. 'Perfect,' she said. 'Let's draw a vampire!"

Jack plucked the magic feather from her hand. 'I think I've got the answer.'

'The answer to what?' said Coco. 'How to draw a vampire?'

'What do you get if you cut a circle in half?' he said, as he turned towards the doors.

'Hey, Jack!' she called. 'Where are you going? The party's only just started.'

tWENtY-FIVE

Jack laid the photo of the school on the library table. 'Okay, Coco – pass me my feather.'

'Yippee! What are you gonna draw?'

'Just you wait.' Jack lowered the nib to the photo – with a sweep of his wrist, he drew a big semi-circle over the roof. He leaned back and folded his arms.

'Z'at it?' Coco squinted at the photo and scrunched up her nose. 'Looks like my granddad's bald patch.'

Jack smiled. 'Yep,' he said. 'That's it. Not bad, eh? I just saved Curtly Ambrose from total environmental devastation.' He opened the window and reached out his hand – a snowflake fluttered down, settled on his palm and was gone. He raised his face to the sky – he could hear a bird singing and see the clouds melting to blue. 'And it's already started working.'

The sun hung over the playground wall, filling the library with rosy light. It glistened on the treetops and shimmered on the ground. The children, the teachers, the mums and the dads were all crowding round the ice-cream van. Mr Waywood was standing on the bonnet.

'*KAA!*' he screeched, flapping his arms.

And one hundred and seventeen penguins raised their heads. They shuffled out of the igloo and dived off the bouncy cupcake, scooting and sliding over the ice. Mr Bodger opened the van door – and pecking and squawking, screeching and flapping, the penguins scrabbled inside.

'Hold on,' said Jack. 'Where's Pablo?'

'Look!' said Coco. 'By the climbing frame.' One last penguin, with orange feet and an orange beak, was waddling towards the van.

'What's happening?' said Jack. 'I – I don't get it. Where are they going?'

'Shh!' Coco lifted her pigtail and leaned out of the library window. 'Mr Waywood's making a speech . . .' Her eyes widened. She shook her head. 'I think he just said *Antarctica*.'

'No way,' said Jack. 'You must've heard it wrong. You need to get your ears cleaned, Coco – there's something blocking your membranes.' He pushed the window open wider and thrust his head outside – he could hear a ripple of clapping and cheers on the warm summer breeze.

'. . . six o'clock ferry . . .' Mr Waywood was saying, '. . . Cape of Good Hope . . . South Pole by Tuesday lunchtime . . .'

Jack looked at Coco – her face was so pale he could count every freckle.

Bang! went the door of the ice-cream van. The children, the teachers and the mums and dads stepped away. A crowd of black-and-white faces was peering through the serving hatch and a huddle of penguins was squatting on the roof. Mr Bodger waded through the sludge with his broom, sweeping a path to the huge wooden gates. He unlocked the padlock and heaved them open.

Jack turned to the door. 'We can't let this happen. I nearly lost him once and I'm not gonna—'

'Too late,' said Coco. 'They're leaving!'

Brmm-brmm-brmm the engine revved and ding-a-ling-ling went the chimes. A jet of spray shot out as the wheels spun and the ice-cream van zigzagged across the playground. Ding-a-ling-ling – it swerved round the bouncy cupcake and skidded away through the gates. Mr Bodger clicked the padlock shut and the children and the mums and dads climbed the steps to the hall.

'Come back!' screamed the tree. 'I'll pull your teeth out one by one! I'll have your molars for breakfast!'

Jack wrapped his scarf around himself and pulled the library window shut.

'You all right?' said Coco. 'Your chin's going wobbly.'

'D'you think he'll be okay?'

'Course he will.' She patted his shoulder. 'Jumping off icebergs and eating plankton? He's gonna have the best time ever.'

'But he's never tried plankton before,' said Jack. 'What if he doesn't like it? Who's gonna make him popcorn? Who's gonna draw him a stuffed-crust pizza?' He felt his throat tighten. His chest gave a shudder. 'N-nobody knows him like we do.'

The sun was sinking behind the school wall and the library was growing darker.

'They'll be on the motorway by now,'

said Coco. 'He's probably forgotten us already.'

Jack slumped into a chair and dug his toe in the carpet. 'He . . . he risked his life for me and I never even said thank you.'

'Huk-huk!'

'I miss him so much I can practically hear him.' Jack gazed across the library – an orange beak was poking round the door, followed by a wing and a round white tummy. 'I can even see him, Coco – it's like he's waddling towards me.'

'Jack, you dog-dollop – he's back!'

Jack sprang out of the chair. 'Pablo? Z'at really you?'

'Huk-huk!' Pablo nodded and waggled his tail.

'Come on.' Jack knelt down. He ruffled Pablo's head and tickled him under the chin. 'I'm taking you home.' He snatched up his feather from the table and twirled it in his hand. 'I'm starving. How about I draw us a paddling pool if I go easy on the toppings?'

'Hukka-hukka-hukka!' went Pablo, hopping from foot to foot.

'Hey, Coco,' he called. 'Get a move on!'

She reached into her pocket then tossed something into the air. It flashed in the evening light as it spun across the library. 'Catch, Pablo!' she cried.

Pablo opened his beak and threw back his head. He gulped and crossed his eyes.

Jack sighed. 'And what was that, exactly?'

''S'no big deal.' Coco shrugged. 'Just the key to the storeroom.'

'You've got to stop doing that, you fruitcake. It's bad for his digestion.'

'Well, I had to hide it somewhere,' she said. 'I've locked Rubella inside.'

ACKNOWLEDGEMENTS

I'd like to thank my editors, Liz Bankes and Susila Baybars, Judy Brown for wielding her magic pen again, and everyone at Catnip Books and Bounce Marketing. Big thanks too, to my friend and agent Ben Illis and the gang of zombie fighters that is Team BIA, to Marcus and Milo, my friends and family, and anyone else who occasionally laughs at my jokes.

ABOUT THE AUTHOR:

Sophie Plowden is five foot eleven
and three quarters.

She likes painting and writing
and teaching art. And salted liquorice.

ABOUT THE ILLUSTRATOR:

Judy Brown has been drawing pictures
(and writing stories) for as long as
she can remember.

She has three children
and lives in Surrey with her illustrator
husband and two stroppy brown cats.

FOR MORE LAUGH OUT LOUD FUNNY BOOKS, FOLLOW THE CAT!

JACK D

AHEM ... FOLLOW THE **CAT** ... (*NOT* THE PIG)

www.catnippublishing.co.uk
Twitter: @catnipbooks